Deadly Undertaking

By J. Q. Rose

Amazon Print 978-0-2286-0927-8

BWL Publishing Inc.

Books we love to write ...
Authors around the world.

http://bwlpublishing.ca

Dedication

To Bernie. My mentor and friend.

Acknowledgement

Special thanks to Tess Grant, W.S. Gager, Joselyn Vaughn, Nan Ross-Flanigan, Sally Kent, Gail Roughton, Roseanne Dowell, and Sandra Rossier, for their input on this story and my brothers Jim and John and sister-in-law Sandy for sharing their experiences in the funeral business. Any errors are my own. Many thanks to cover artist Michelle Lee for the book cover design and publisher Jude Pittman of Books We Love.

Chapter One

"Lauren, quick, call 9-1-1, there's a dead body out here in the garage!"

Dad and his bad jokes. This is a funeral home. Of course there's a body here.

"Lauren, did you hear me? Call 9-1-1."

Hearing the urgency in his voice, Lauren grabbed her cell phone from the desk, kicked off her high heels, and ran toward the garage.

Lauren skidded to a stop in the doorway. A man lay sprawled face down in a pool of blood on the garage floor between the black funeral coach and SUV. Her father looked up and shook his head. Bile rose to her throat, and she turned away from the ghastly scene.

Trying to steady her hands long enough to punch in 9-1-1, she breathed deeply and squeezed her eyes shut to block the image from her mind.

"What is your emergency?" a nasal voice on the phone asked.

"There's a man in our garage. I think he's dead." Her voice sounded unusually loud and high pitched.

"What's your name and location?"

"Lauren Staab, Staab and Blood Funeral Home, 405 East Main Street."

"Is this a joke? If this is a prank call, there are serious consequences, Ma'am."

"No, no. It's true. There's a dead man on the floor of our garage." Lauren's stomach churned. "Hurry, call the police." She knew she was going to be sick. "Get the police here now!" Clamping her hand over her mouth, she raced for the other side of the funeral coach.

* * *

Lauren lay on the couch in the family room of the funeral home. She rubbed her temples, but neither that nor squeezing her head relieved the pressure of the banging like a jackhammer in her brain.

Sure she grew up in the funeral home business, but her dad never let her in the embalming room even to this day. Her job was in the office and helping out with visitations and conducting services. She was never around a body until the person was in the casket, dressed, made-up, and hair styled. She shuddered when she remembered the gory sight in the garage.

After her call the police had swarmed in and around the building, blocking off the garage with yellow tape. An officer had escorted her into the family room with instructions to stay there. Lauren was glad to be away from the action. It looked like some crime scene investigation show she'd watched on TV. It couldn't be happening here, right now. But the scene must be real, not a TV production. No movie-star type detectives at this crime scene.

She watched the coming and goings of so many personnel and caught a glimpse of the ambulance through the window as it slowly trundled out of the driveway onto Main St. No need to hurry. It was too late to save the occupant.

Lauren winced at the irony of the situation. Usually vehicles brought dead bodies *in* via the driveway.

She sighed. She needed a cigarette and some aspirin.

"Here, hon." Her dad handed her a cold, wet washcloth. Pressing the cloth to her forehead, she sat up to face him.

Jensen handed his pale daughter a glass of water. "Thank you." Lauren felt like a frightened child again, but at this point she didn't care. She was relieved to know her dad was there for her.

Her father sat down next to her on the couch. The tastefully appointed room featured overstuffed couches and warm neutral colors to give comfort to family members who had lost their loved one. Right now it was a safe place for the father and daughter to keep out of the way of the police investigation.

"How're you feeling?" Her dad's gray eyes studied her face.

"I'm doing as well as one could expect after a morning like this one." She flashed a weak smile.

"Too bad they had to take the man's body to the medical examiner. We could've saved them a lot of trouble and money if we'd loaded him into our embalming room." Her dad's eyes twinkled with that weak attempt to lighten the moment.

"Yeah, Dad, but who would I send the bill to?" she countered.

"Always the practical bookkeeper." He patted her knee.

"Well somebody's got to think about the money in this business." She took another sip of water. Her stomach was not as queasy, and the water glass wasn't shaking in her grip.

Lauren pushed off the couch to return to her desk in the office across the hall. "Well, since we have to hang around here for questions, I'm going to finish up those invoices. Hopefully we'll be able to leave for lunch. Do you want to join me at the Koffee Kuppe for a bowl of our favorite cheese soup?" She hoped her voice sounded normal to let her dad know she was better now.

"No, thanks. I'm just having coffee here. I have to meet with the Jackson family at two this afternoon. You go ahead." He stood up and hugged her. Lauren breathed in the familiar smell of cigarette smoke and spicy cologne, bringing back childhood memories when she always felt safe in his arms.

Stepping back from him, she caught the concerned look on his face. He asked, "You okay now?"

"I'll be fine. Don't worry about me." She wrinkled her nose. "I wonder how long they'll take checking out our garage, now known as the crime scene." She wiggled her fingers in the air to make quotes around crime scene.

"Sorry, Sis, I'm a funeral director. Not a cop. I'm sure this isn't the end of the story though."

Lauren ran her fingers through her blonde hair and tugged the hem of her blouse down over the top of her navy blue slacks. Thank goodness she'd missed her clothing when she tossed her cookies by the hearse.

"I don't believe they've identified the man." He shrugged. "Do you know him?"

"I didn't recognize him, but I didn't really look too closely." Lauren gazed down at the floor and noticed her bare toes on the carpet. Way too overwhelmed to think of anything like her shoes still in her office in the aftermath of the discovery of the body, she wrinkled her brow wondering what else she forgot.

* * *

Lauren settled into her comfortable leather chair behind the cherry wood desk in the office. Elbows on the desk and holding her aching head, she tried to erase the memory of the man in the garage. She had moved from the CPA accounting firm in Grand Rapids to help her dad four years ago. She wasn't supposed to be finding bodies on the garage floor. She shuddered at the image stuck in her mind.

She glanced at her mother's portrait on the desk and choked back the lump in her throat. Her beautiful mother was doing well in the nursing home, but every day the dementia attacked her brain, and the mom she knew was disappearing. *Oh, Mom, how I wish you were here to help us through this.*

The jangling desk phone startled Lauren out of her thoughts. "Hello. Staab and Blood Funeral Home. This is Lauren."

"Lauren. I just heard about the murder at the funeral home. Are you all right? Do you want me to come over?"

Lauren frowned. Covering her disappointment, she answered in her best brightest voice. "Oh, hi, Emmett. I'm fine. A murder?" Lauren hadn't allowed herself time to face the fact the actual crime of murder had been committed in their garage. Her stomach flipped at the thought.

"Hell, everyone's talking about it. I'm going to come over now to be with you. I'll be there right away."

"Oh, uh, that's thoughtful of you, but I'm leaving here soon to, uh, go lie down. I'm a little jumpy. No need for you to come over now."

"Are you sure? 'Cause I'd be happy to come on over---."

Lauren cut him off. "Thanks, but, no. That's very thoughtful of you. I'll talk to ya'

10

later." Lauren bit her lip. She hated lying. Emmett was one of those guys who didn't get the message. She had no interest in him. If he weren't one of her brother's friends, she would have cut off ties to Emmett a long time ago.

"Well, hey, can I talk to Randy?"

"Randy's not here right now. But I'll give him the message you called. Bye."

She quickly placed the burgundy phone in the cradle to guarantee the end of the conversation.

If only it would be that easy to end this long day of horror.

* * *

Someone tapped on the partially opened office door. "Excuse me, Lauren. Can I come in?"

The door opened a little farther and a familiar face peered around it.

Lauren's eyes opened wide in surprise. "Oh, Gary, yes, please. Come in." She stood up to greet the tall policeman. "I never thought I'd see you here." She smiled at her old high school classmate as he stepped into the office.

"Well that makes two of us."

"What's up, Goose?" She used the nickname he had in school, earned way back in seventh grade when he supposedly goosed another player on the opposing basketball team in the last remaining seconds of the game, so the kid punched him. Gary fell to the floor. The referee never saw the goose and called a technical on the boy. The team won the game when Gary made the free throw.

Lauren swept her eyes up and down to take in the new buff body in his police uniform. He had certainly changed from the skinny nerdy guy who helped her with her trigonometry assignments in high school

She grasped his hand in a firm handshake and held on for a bit longer than she needed to. "I heard you were back here on the Mayfield police force. It's good to see you again. Not so much in these circumstances though."

"I hope I'm not interrupting you. Just wanted to check and see how you're holding up."

"I'm okay. Kind of worried about Dad. The older he gets the less stress he can handle." She noticed Gary studying her face intensely. Did he think she was going to fall apart in front of him?

"To tell you the truth, someone said it's a murder investigation. Now my mind is whirling with possibilities. Do you think whoever killed that man will be back to kill us?" Her voice cracked. She'd been thinking about it after Emmett's call, but actually saying it out loud frightened her even more. What if the killer was looking for her dad, Randy, or for her? Would he come back?

Gary put his arm around her shoulders and turned his face to look directly into her eyes. "Well, believe me, we have plenty of police on the premises. Nobody's going to be here to harm you or your dad. We'll have twenty-four-hour patrols watching this place." He stepped away and resumed his policeman-like interrogation. The change in his manner jarred her a bit. Their friendship went back many years, but today he was focused on the job he had to do, to find a killer.

"Your mom and dad live in the second story of the funeral home. Are you and your brother residing upstairs too?" His brow creased "We need to know where your family is since we'll patrol the area till we get some answers here."

"No, I have my own place on Lake St. My brother and dad still live here, but Mom's out at the nursing home in the Memory Care unit now."

"Oh, I'm sorry to hear that." His tone of voice was soft and sincere.

"Well, you recently moved back here. It'll take a while to get caught up with all the hometown news." She motioned to the chair in front of the desk. "Please have a seat and I'll fill you in on all the gossip."

"Thanks, but I can't right now. Maybe we can go for coffee and catch up sometime." He winked at her. "I wanted to check on you. If you need anything or have questions, here's my card." He handed it to her. "Really, Lauren. Please call me any time day or night. I mean it." His face was so serious. She remembered the same intense look when he helped her with her trig homework. He always made sure she understood each problem before he'd let her move on to the next one.

"I'm good. Much better now to know the police will be around here. I think that'll help Dad too. Thanks."

"Okay. You take care now, Lauren." He grinned at her, turned around, and left, leaving the door ajar just as it was when he first knocked. She looked after him, sorry to see him leave so soon. It would have been fun to remember the "good old days" with him. She needed some laughs right now.

Lauren sat back down at her desk and stared at her computer screen trying to gather her thoughts and concentrate on the work at hand. She felt better now knowing Gary and the police would be watching the place.

Still, the thought niggled her mind. *Is a killer stalking me?*

Chapter Two

"Yes, Detective. My daughter's in the office this afternoon. Please follow me."

Her father's voice sounded through the open door. Cramming another file in her To Do basket on the corner of her desk, she tried to tidy up her desk before the visitor entered.

When she looked up, she was pleasantly surprised to see a tall, fine-looking man standing in the doorway. Having grown up in Mayfield, she pretty much knew everyone in the small farming community. If she had seen this guy in town, she definitely would've noticed him.

Perhaps she was correct recalling her first impression that she'd been dreaming about the crime scene being a movie set. With his good looks, this man certainly fit the heroic Hollywood detective character.

"Lauren, this is Detective Richards. He's here for information about..."

"Thank you, Mr. Staab. I can take it from here." The detective turned from her father and faced Lauren. She stood and walked around her desk, her gaze never dropping from his face. She had never seen such startling blue eyes in her life. She was mesmerized by his deeply tanned skin and wavy dark hair.

"Hello, Ms. Staab. May I come in?" His smile revealed polished white teeth with a front tooth tilted ever so slightly. He could definitely come into her office and into her life. Lauren extended her hand to the detective, but he did not grasp it, only nodded.

"Nice to meet you, Detective Richards." She grinned at him and felt like a thirteen-year-old girl whose crush actually noticed her.

"Dad, come on in. I have enough chairs here for everyone." Lauren stood back from the door and swept her arm toward the room.

Turning to face her father, Detective Richards said, "No, Mr. Staab. I've already gotten your story on what happened this morning. Now I'd like to interview Ms. Staab."

"Of course. I'll be in my office if you have any further questions." The solemn look on his face made Lauren wonder how his interview went with this serious detective.

Lauren closed the door to the office. "You can keep the door open," Richards said.

"Oh, sure." She opened the heavy four-paneled wooden door and motioned to the detective to have a seat in the upholstered chair across from her desk. He waited for her to go around her desk and sit down before he took his seat.

"Thank you for your time this afternoon. This is a preliminary investigation into the death of the victim in the garage." His eyes practically drilled into her soul. He quickly flashed his badge proving he was from the Mayfield Police Department and handed her his business card.

Lauren took the card and glanced at it. Her hands trembled, so she pitched it onto her desk and hid her hands in her lap.

"Okay, let's start from the beginning. He pulled a small notebook and pen from his pocket and casually leaned against the back of the chair as if he were going to watch TV instead of waiting to hear about a dead man in the garage. Lauren sucked in a deep breath and began relating the events of the morning. His eyes remained fixed on her as she recounted her experience. At times he quickly scribbled a note in his notebook, then faced her again revealing no emotion in those dark blue eyes. She couldn't read his thoughts. She squirmed a bit in her chair. It was hard to concentrate on the events because her heart seemed to be skipping beats when she gazed into his eyes.

After listening to Lauren for nearly half an hour and interrupting her for a few clarifications, the detective said, "Thank you, Ms. Staab. We may have a few questions for you later at the police station."

"At the police station? Why's that?" Her eyes darkened at the thought of having to re-tell the horrible experience yet another time.

"I said we *may* have a few more questions. That's all." His manner was courteous as he stood.

Lauren walked around her desk. "Fine, Detective, I'm willing to co-operate with the investigation. I'll be available anytime…to answer your questions. I didn't mean I was available any time, I mean, you know…I have a boyfriend. Oh, but he wasn't here this morning." Lauren shook her head. Her face burned with embarrassment. How was she going to dig herself out of this hole?

A hint of a smile flashed across the rugged face. Lauren was delighted he could smile and show a little emotion even if it was at her expense.

"If you think of anything you want to add, please call me."

When he turned to leave, Lauren admired his broad shoulders under the navy blue sports coat nearly pursing her lips for a whistle of appreciation for this guy.

Sheesh. She collapsed into her chair and lowered her head in her hands. Talk about making a fool of herself. Perspiration soaked her blouse and dizziness overcame her.

What made her tell him she had a boyfriend? She thought of Chip DeYoung. He was the closest thing to a boyfriend she had. But she wasn't giddy about him and didn't yearn to be with him every minute of the day.

As far as Lauren was concerned, she truly had no boyfriend, no knight in shining armor, no one to love, and no one who truly loved her back. Well, except for her dad and her brother, Randy. So pitiful.

Lauren settled into her chair and stared at the computer screen. She couldn't focus long

18

enough to get any work done. The images of the morning's events and Detective Richards swirled through her brain until her brother burst through the doorway.

"What the hell happened here this morning?" Randy pushed into the office. "Are you okay? Where's Dad?"

Lauren practically jumped out of her chair. "I'm fine. Calm down. Dad's okay. He's here. Where've you been?" She scooted back in the big chair, her heart pounding. She'd had enough surprises for one day.

She smiled as she saw her brother's concerned face. Randy's brown eyes were the opposite color of Lauren's sparkling blue eyes. He was blessed with a tall, thin frame which made him a standout on his high school basketball squad many years ago.

Lauren's curvy figure stood a full six inches shorter than her brother. He was the one with brown curly hair and long eyelashes. She got the straight thick hair which barely brushed her shoulders.

"I ran down to Grand Rapids to pick up some motorcycle parts today. I finally got a day off. Remember?" He folded himself in the chair across from her desk.

The funeral business seemed to follow the old saying that deaths come in three. They were either busier than a cat covering up, or languishing with no business at all. If only people could die at decent intervals, it would be so much easier for the undertakers.

"Emmett called me about the excitement here this morning. He said he heard at the Koffee Kuppe that some guy got popped and Dad dragged him into the garage and was going to claim him. He didn't want the cops to take him to another funeral home in town." Randy laughed. "The other rumor is that the guy was your boyfriend and Dad didn't like him, so he shot him."

"No way. No waaaaay." Lauren scowled at the tale made up out of whole cloth. That's the way it was in small towns. The gossip reminded her of the days when she was a little girl and her friends played "Telephone." One girl would whisper a sentence in another girl's ear. That girl would whisper what she thought she heard to the next girl. By the time the last girl repeated the sentence out loud, it was not even close to the original. The game was always a barrel of laughs for the players. But this exaggeration of the murder this morning wasn't a laughing matter.

"I don't think they've even identified the guy yet. Oh, Randy, it was so sickening. He was sprawled on the cement garage floor with his face blown away." She shook her head to clear out the ghastly image in her mind. Tears welled up in her eyes, but she scrubbed them away with her hands before her brother could see her cry.

"Hey, hey. Are you okay?" Randy moved from his chair, knelt down by his sister and hugged her. It felt good, but completely out of character for her tough brother.

"I, I…" The blubbering hit her so hard she couldn't speak. All of a sudden the events poured in on her. She could no longer be strong and aloof from the horror she had witnessed. She clung to Randy knowing she was getting the front of his Harley tee-shirt all wet, but not caring.

Randy pulled a tissue from the box on her desk, available for grieving family members to use when needed. She accepted it and wiped her eyes and blew her nose. She needed another.

He stood up and said, "You look like hell." Well now, that was more like her brother. "You need to go home."

"I don't want to go home. I need to keep busy here so I don't think about it. Just look at what happened now when I remembered it all." She wiped her nose again and threw the tissues in the waste basket behind her. They both hit the target.

Randy patted her shoulders returned to sit in the chair. He crossed one long blue-jeaned leg over the other. "There's some talk that the dead man in the garage was Ronnie Bell."

Lauren bit her lip as she wondered why anyone would murder him. "Ronnie Bell? But he's such a sweet guy with a darling wife and I think three or four kids. All girls." Lauren grabbed another tissue from the box and wiped her eyes and dabbed her nose.

"How's Dad doing," he asked. Lauren saw the worry in his face.

"I know he's trying to be strong for my sake. Actually I haven't had much of a chance to talk to him. We've been separated talking to the police. I did see him when he brought the detective to my office a while ago."

"What? The police are questioning you? Surely they don't think you had anything to do with this!" Randy sat straight up in the chair.

"Hey, Dad yelled for me when he found the body. So of course I was involved. You have no idea what we went through."

Lauren placed her palms on the desk. "Detective Richards told me he may have me come to the police station if there are any more questions."

"Detective Richards, eh? I think he's new here. I haven't met him yet. Some of the guys have talked about him."

"Really? What'd they say?" She leaned in toward her brother.

"Huh? Oh I didn't pay much attention to it."

"Well, is he married, got kids? Where's he from?"

Randy grinned. "You seem pretty interested in this guy. What's up?"

Lauren averted her eyes from her questioning brother and flipped a look toward the desk and faced Randy again. "I was just curious. He asked me all kinds of questions. I thought I'd find out about him too." She folded her arms across her chest, noticing the mischief in her brother's eyes.

He arched an eyebrow. "Well, Sis, I'll find out more for you, and I won't even mention this to Chip." He stood up and leaned toward her. "Are you up for a cup of coffee now?"

"I sure am! Only if you make it and put in half the coffee you usually measure out. I don't want the spoon to stand up all by itself in the cup of mud."

Now why did he have to go and mention Chip? As Randy disappeared into the hallway, Lauren yelled, "By the way, it's none of Chip's business anyway."

Chapter Three

"You still there at the funeral home?" Lauren recognized her friend Piper's familiar voice on the phone.

"Yes, I'm here." Lauren held the cell phone closer to her ear. She took one last puff, then threw the cigarette butt near the bushes outside the funeral home, ground it into the dirt, and buried it.

"Oh, my God, Lauren, are you okay? What the hell happened? I couldn't believe what I heard just now!" Her best friend's voice ratcheted up higher with every word.

"What did you hear? You mean about the murder in the garage?"

"Well, yes, about the murder in the garage, Doofus. Stop joking around. I heard it was Tony." Piper's voice cracked.

Lauren swung the phone away from her face as she covered her swirling stomach with her other hand. Wouldn't she have recognized Tony? No. She avoided looking at what was left of the demolished face on the body in the garage.

"What? Tony?" Lauren's eyes darkened. Tony VanZant was their friend Stephanie's fiancé.

"Well, I tried calling Stephanie, but there's no answer. I thought you may've heard something. We need to talk."

Lauren took a deep breath to gain some time to absorb the idea that the dead man could be a friend.

"Lauren. Are you there?" Piper's voice brought her back to reality. "Are you okay?"

Straightening her posture, Lauren gripped the phone firmly in her hand like she was hanging on to a lifeline.

"Well, sure. Where and when do you want to meet? You're the one with two kids."

"Ray'll be home soon. I've got the macaroni and cheese made and will fly out the door, changing of the guard so-to-speak, and meet you at The Rat in half an hour. Will that work for you?"

"That's perfect. I'll finish up here and go on over." Tears blossomed in Lauren's eyes without warning. "I'm so glad you called, Piper." The knot in her throat made it impossible to even say good-bye, so Lauren ended the call knowing her best friend since second grade would understand.

Gathering her wits about her, Lauren decided she needed to know if the dead man truly was Tony. If so, she and Piper had to find Stephanie.

She returned to her desk, uncovered Detective Richards' business card from under the files on her desk, and called.

"Richards." he answered as if he had no time for interruptions.

Lauren was taken aback for a minute, expecting a secretary or switchboard person to answer and connect her to the detective.

"Hello, Detective Richards. This is Lauren Staab, at the Staab and Blood Funeral Home where the murder occurred this morning." She stalled for enough time to get her thoughts together.

"Yes, I'm quite aware the murder was at the funeral home, Ms. Staab. How can I help you?"

What an arrogant man. "I'm calling to confirm the identity of the person who was killed. I've heard several reports."

"We're not revealing the name of the deceased."

"Well can you tell me if his name is Tony?"

"Sorry. I cannot." His voice softened. "I'm not at liberty at this time to tell you. I completely understand your concern. Do you know Anthony—er. Tony?"

"Yes, I do. He's my friend's fiancé."

"I know the rumor mill is probably producing more names than this, but we have to be sure of the victim's identity before we release it. Do you understand the situation?" Lauren detected a note of sincerity in his voice. Did the man have feelings after all?

"Oh, yes I understand. But since he was in our garage, will someone call me to let me know?" She couldn't help using the snarky tone.

"Yes. I'll be sure to call you as soon as we have a definitive identification. You have a good evening." The phone clicked to silence.

"And you have a good night too!" She slammed the head set into the cradle, yanked the desk drawer open, and retrieved her bag. She didn't like being dismissed like that.

She reached into her bag to find her pack of cigarettes, pulled it out, threw it back in, and pulled the beat up pack out again. So much for trying once more to quit smoking.

When she looked up, she glimpsed a smoky shadow hovering by the door. The pungent smell of spicy carnations wafted through the room, bringing on the three little sneezes. She worked in a funeral home. She shouldn't be allergic to flowers. Maybe she was allergic to him.

Lauren faced the silhouette of a man dressed in a long trench coat and fedora hat. He stood, arms akimbo, evidently looking straight at her.

She had expected the shadow man to show up sometime after the terrifying events of the morning. He lurked around the rooms in the funeral home appearing whenever he wished. Because no one else ever mentioned the apparition, Lauren assumed she was the only one he communicated with. At times she questioned if Henry was real or just her overtired brain playing tricks on her.

His timing for wanting to talk was usually bad. This murder was definitely a bad time.

"Henry, I can't talk now. I'm leaving to meet Piper." She shoved the drawer closed with her foot.

"All right," he said in his breathy voice. "I guess you're doing okay if you can go off to meet your friend." Then he was gone, slipping through a fold into another dimension.

Chapter Four

Lauren stood to greet Piper when she entered The Rathskeller known as "the Rat" to locals. The restaurant was one of the hangouts drawing in the residents of Mayfield. The name never changed over all the years, but the owners did. Presently the restaurant sported a Western theme with blaring country music adding to the casual atmosphere. They were known for their craft beer and tasty burritos and burgers, comfort food to fill her sorrowful heart.

Piper grabbed Lauren for a hug. Lauren swore Piper gave the best hugs ever. Her big brown eyes looked troubled. "Hey, quit worrying. I'm fine. Sit down and let's chomp down on some good food."

They scooted into the brown naugahyde-covered booth and sat across from each other. Lauren faced her friend. Even after giving birth to twins, Piper bounced back into the slim, petite girl Lauren had known most of her life. Her long dark hair was pulled back into one of those mom hair-dos, no time for fussing with a blow dryer or flat iron. The style actually accentuated her attractive face.

Immediately the roly-poly waitress came to the table to take their order. More likely, she wanted to find out about the murder. "Oh, my gosh, Lauren. What a day you've had, eh?" She rolled her eyes and looked like she was ready to burst if she didn't hear the entire story.

"Yeah, it's been a tough one. I'll take your light beer and an order of nachos," Lauren said. "You having your usual red wine, Piper?"

"Um, yes, I guess and...I'll wait to order something later. Thanks."

The waitress waited a bit, anticipating a telling of the events of the day, but when Lauren said nothing else, she stomped off to turn in the order.

"Are you sure you're okay? You always order a burrito." Piper put her hand out to cover Lauren's.

"Oh, stop worrying. I'm fine. No nightmares tonight. The police are handling it." She hoped she sounded convincing. Lauren fished around for her pack of cigarettes, but remembered, no smoking in public places. She threw it back into her bag and turned her attention to Piper ready to unload her day onto her best friend, the best listener ever. She began by relating the discovery of the body, the police and medical examiner's investigations, and finally the visit by the gruff, but gorgeous, Detective Richards.

When the waitress toddled over with the drinks, Lauren waited until she was out of listening range before she continued her story. With the music and the crowd noise, she could talk without being overheard.

"I called the detective, but he wouldn't tell me anything. I suppose he may not know for sure. He's new in town. Not really knowing anyone, he doesn't know he could trust me with the information."

"Well, I hope he has some cops watching your place." Piper reached for her wine glass for a sip of red wine.

"Funny you should mention that. Remember Gary Applegate? Goose?" Piper wrinkled her brow, then her eyes lit up with name recognition.

"Yeah, I remember. Oh, right, he's back in town on the city police force. Was he there this morning?"

"He's the one who came in to tell me they would be patrolling the funeral home and my apartment to keep us safe."

Piper's mouth turned up into a smile. "That's a relief to know you'll be protected. You know what I mean. They don't know why that guy was murdered and why in the world he would be dumped at your place. Come on. Think about it. They could have dumped him in the river or the woods or even at Swartz's Funeral Home across town. Why did he end up at Staab and Blood?"

"Oh, no. Not Swartz. They do terrible work there!" Piper didn't smile.

"I don't want to worry you, hon but there *is* a reason for their picking your place. Maybe because Randy knows the man? Maybe your Dad had dealings with the dead guy?"

31

The waitress interrupted the conversation by placing the pile of nachos in the center of the table. "Okay, gals, I'll be back in a few to see if you need anything else."

Lauren's stomach turned over at the sight of the gooey cheese and sauce on the pile of tortilla chips. Could her brother or her dad be in danger? And what if she were the reason? She shook her head to erase the troubling thoughts. Why was her friend Piper still the smart one like she was since second grade?

The cell phone's muffled tune played in the side pocket of her bag erasing all thoughts of the dead man in the funeral home garage. Lauren hoped it was the detective, but when she found the jangling phone, the caller ID was Stephanie's.

"It's Stephanie," she whispered as she punched the button on the phone. "Hello."

"Tony. It was Tony. Somebody killed him." Stephanie's voice dissolved into sobs.

"Oh dear God, Stephanie. It was Tony?" Tears instantly sprang into Lauren's eyes. What do you say to your friend? What can you say when you were the witness to her fiancé's bloody body sprawled out in your garage? Lauren thought she was going to throw up. She handed the phone to Piper and grabbed a tissue from her bag holding it over her mouth to staunch the bile gathering in her throat.

"Stephanie, it's Piper. We'll be right over. Are you at the house?"

"No, I'm leaving the M.E.'s office. I had to identify….." She couldn't continue.

"I am so sorry, hon." Piper took a deep breath. "Okay, are you going home now? We'll meet you there. Is that okay?"

Piper nodded her head as she listened. "We'll meet you at your place. We'll be there waiting for you. I am so sorry. So sorry."

Piper passed the phone back to Lauren and grabbed the napkin to wipe her teary eyes and blow her nose.

"We need to go now. Let's go, Piper." Lauren shoved her phone back in her bag and retrieved another tissue. She breathed deeply, then stood and waited while Piper collected her things from the booth. Her stomach was still doing flip flops and her head ached, but she could only imagine the loss, sorrow, and grief Stephanie felt. The questions with no answers.

Who would kill Tony, that funny and kind man? Why would anyone want to hurt him? No one should get away with killing her friend's fiancé. She didn't have the answers, but she was going to do anything she could to help find the murderer.

Chapter Five

After a sleepless night filled with scenes of seeing the body and dealing with police who wore SWAT team gear, Lauren arrived at the funeral home tired and worried about her dad. She had called him last night and he assured her he was okay. Randy lived in the apartment on the second floor of the funeral home with him, but would Randy notice if her dad needed her?

Fretting too much about her father, Lauren parked her Kia in the east lot near the side door of the funeral home. On her way to work she decided not to enter the building through the back door that led through the garage. The thought of picturing the inside of the garage with the body, Tony's body, lying there brought back yesterday's horrible morning of madness. Her stomach clenched at the memories.

Lauren gathered her bag and lunch tote from the back seat and slammed the car door, not noticing what a beautiful summer morning it was. Pressing the button on the remote to lock her car, she turned to walk the short distance to the entry door.

On a usual work day morning, she would take a minute to appreciate the Victorian era house painted in its historically correct colors of cream with slate blue trim. The modern addition was cleverly designed to keep the flavor of the bygone period. Added about ten years ago, the area offered a larger chapel seating area and better facilities for logistically moving the bodies from the added garage to the embalming room.

Two cars entered the driveway that led behind the funeral home and attached garage. She watched occupants of the cars rubber-neck as they crept past the closed garage doors. She wanted to jump out in front of the car and scream at the curiosity seekers bold enough to drive on the property strictly for a look-see of the crime scene. *Can't they see I am standing here watching them?*

The two-story house sat at the corner of Main and Maple. The driveway intersected Maple St, the side street, so it was easy for anyone to turn in and go past the garage attached to the building. She watched the vehicles enter the large parking lot on the west side of the funeral home where they could exit via the entrance off Main St.

Lauren rolled her eyes realizing the sightseers would be driving by all day. Much like a car wreck or the aftermath of a tornado, evidently the scene of a crime attracts the curious too.

As she entered the side door into the family room, Lauren placed her bag and lunch on the counter. Her stomach turned over with the thought of drinking a cup of coffee, but she needed to do something to energize her after a long sleepless night. She couldn't settle down after last night's meeting with Stephanie.

"Stephanie. Stephanie." Words of condolence stuck in her throat when she faced the raw grief etched on her friend's face. Lauren clasped her in her arms and they both shook with sobs and heartache. Although she had helped many families who had lost loved ones to cancer, accidents, and suicide, she didn't have the words to express her deep sorrow and loss to her close friend.

Dealing with the death of a friend, no matter how it happened, was nearly impossible. This senseless murder enraged her.

Lauren wiped away her tears, wanting to take her mind off of Stephanie and her shattered life. She had to face a new day.

Lauren pulled out the soft dusting cloth from the stash of cleaning supplies in the closet. She walked with purpose to the casket room where eight caskets of various colors were displayed on rolling biers.

Lauren had been polishing the caskets since she was old enough to hold a dust cloth. Making them shine gave her a sense of accomplishment and pride.

The fragrance of wood, new material, and furniture polish greeted her before she switched on the overhead lights to illuminate the large room housing the caskets and a corner set aside to display urns for cremains. The head of every casket was open so the family coming in this afternoon could see the colors and feel the soft interiors with a matching pillow and stole. Usually the units were closed to keep the interiors clean.

The many choices of color combinations, materials, and prices rivaled the choices for choosing carpeting or paint for a house. Jensen only displayed some of the more popular lines so the selection didn't overwhelm the families. They faced so many decisions after losing a loved one and this was always a difficult one to make.

Lauren unfolded the soft cloth and dusted off the shiny blue metallic casket with the silver accents hoping the familiar work would help her stop worrying about the people she loved. She rubbed harder to make the casket gleam under the soft ceiling lights. The mundane task usually relaxed her, and she felt herself calm as she worked her way around the room.

She eyed the rich oak casket as the next project. Its soft beige interior added to the classiness of the piece. Without thinking, she smoothed the inside of the casket checking how soft the mattress could be. So many times the family made the final decision on which casket to choose because they wanted the one that would be comfortable for their loved one to rest in for eternity.

As she dusted the foot of the casket her cloth caught on the corner. That was unusual. No sharp edges were ever on these well-crafted pieces. After looking closer, she noticed the foot was unlatched and the cleaning cloth had slipped into the narrow opening between the top and the base. She pulled the lid up and pushed it down to catch on the latch making it fit snug and smooth, a necessity for folks to know that the casket was tight enough to keep out the insects and water.

When she stepped back to survey the room, the caskets gleamed and her anxiety had calmed. She was ready now to enjoy a hot cup of coffee.

Lauren checked her watch and decided it was too early to go upstairs to the apartment. Dad and Randy were probably still sleeping after their own restless night. She'd have coffee in the family room.

As Lauren measured the coffee grounds into the coffee basket, the air temperature changed from comfortable to cold in the room. Goose bumps prickled up her arms and her nose tickled with the spicy scent of white carnations. She buried her nose in the bend of her elbow as three little sneezes in quick succession erupted. She didn't have to look up from her task because all the indicators signaled Henry's presence in the room. She measured the water into the carafe, poured it into the machine, punched the button, and turned to find the shadow man.

His smoky gray silhouette drifted near the cream colored wall. "Good morning, Henry."

"Lauren." The shadow figure tipped his hat and bowed in greeting. Lauren wasn't sure if she actually heard his voice in the room or if it was only in her head.

"I don't suppose you were around here when Tony was dumped in the garage," Lauren asked.

"I'm sorry, dear. I wasn't." He shook his head and moved the umbrella, she often saw him carry, from his right hand to the left one and leaned on it.

"Why? Were you partying down with your spirit friends in the cemetery or flying between heaven and hell?"

The shadow raised his shoulders. "I wish I could help. I wish I knew what happened, but unlike people think, I can't be everywhere at once."

Lauren, placing her hands on her hips, raised her voice. "Why *are* you here? Why do you keep hanging around the funeral home? Just go away. Go away and leave me alone." She motioned him away. "I'm having a very bad day and you, you're not helping." She spun around and grabbed her bag and lunch from the counter. Taking a deep breath, guilt for being so abrupt with Henry washed over her. She turned back to apologize, but he was gone.

"I'm sorry, Henry. I'm so damn tired and angry and depressed." She looked upward hoping to see him, but no sign of his shadow. Perhaps he was still there. The morning sun was so bright shining through the windows, maybe she couldn't see him. She knew that wasn't true.

He had appeared to her in well-lighted rooms as well as dark rooms.

She grimaced with the memory of their first encounter right after they had moved her mom into the nursing home two years ago. Leaving her mother there alone was difficult for all of them. Knowing they could visit anytime and that she would be receiving the excellent care she needed wasn't enough to console them.

"Come on home with us, Sis," her dad said as they left the nursing home that afternoon.

She went home with him and Randy because they needed to support each other. Their emotions were similar to the grief someone felt after a loved one died. In truth, they had lost her before this moment. Through the cruel reality of Alzheimer's disease, the woman they knew as wife and mother disappeared before their eyes every day.

That evening, when her father and Randy received a call to pick up a body, she had gone to her office and sat at her desk, trying to empty her mind of seeing her mother in that nursing home setting. She wanted to kiss away the confusion and fright on her mother's face. But she couldn't. At that moment she heard a voice in the office.

"Don't be afraid, Lauren." The sound jolted her out of her office chair. There was no one in the room, and yet the voice was right in her ear. She felt the chill in the air and her nose tickled a bit from the spicy fragrance in the room.

She grabbed her desk and hung on to catch herself in case she fainted. But no, she wasn't faint. She pinched herself to make sure she wasn't dreaming. She stood up to search every corner of the office for someone hiding in the room until she caught sight of the dark shadow of a man floating near the door. Her heart banged around in her chest, and she forgot to breathe.

"Don't be frightened," the mellow sounding voice intoned. "I'm not here to hurt you. I just want to check on you. I know you and your dad are having a tough time giving your mother up to the nursing home care."

Lauren's knees wouldn't hold her any longer and she fell into the leather chair. Keeping her gaze on the shadowy intruder, she grabbed her bag and dug out her phone to call 9-1-1.

"No need to call for help, Lauren. I'm leaving. Please know, I don't want to hurt you."

She sat transfixed watching the shadow. She clutched the phone in her fist ready to use it as a club if necessary. What should she do? Call 9-1-1 and them what that a spirit was talking to her? They'd haul her off.

She shook her head and sneezed three quick, little sneezes. Damn carnations! She grabbed a tissue from the box ready to catch another sneeze. When she looked up, the shadow had disappeared.

This first meeting was shocking, but eventually Henry became a regular visitor and their visits became normal conversations. Unfortunately he often picked the wrong times to come around. He didn't seem to mind if she was working hard late at night or watching TV at home, or even if she was making out with her boyfriend, Chip. It seemed Henry was oblivious to her situation never considering how his intrusions into her life affected her.

Lauren couldn't help but smile. Although he was a pain in the neck when he showed up at the wrong times, she kind of thought of him as her guardian angel. He was always there whether she needed him or not. She still wondered. Guardian angel or bothersome ghost?

Chapter Six

After parking in her driveway, Lauren retrieved her mail from the mailbox, and approached her front door. Loaded down with her large leather bag on one shoulder and her tablet in one hand, she shoved her mail under her armpit to have a free hand to unlock her front door. She was so glad to finally be home after a long day. Dealing with the day after the murder was nearly as difficult as the previous day. The investigation, the calls from concerned friends and family, the calls from nosey friends, and still trying to take care of business were too much for her to handle. Her emotions were fragile, but she still had to appear strong for her dad's sake.

Lauren glimpsed the police car as it passed her duplex. She looked closely to see if Gary was driving, but evidently not or he would have stopped. Well, maybe he would have. She wasn't sure if he could stop and talk to old friends while on duty. It was lucky she had no neighbors in the other part of the duplex. They probably wouldn't appreciate the police checking the place day and night.

Mayfield had entered the twenty-first century by finally allowing construction companies to build apartments and duplexes in the sleepy town. More and more families were moving into the area to get away from the city and to enjoy the country air, albeit when the wind blew from the wrong direction, some of the country air smelled like cow barns if the new residents bought a place too close to the farms.

Lauren dumped every item she carried onto the table in the entry way. Of course, the junk mail fluttered down to the laminated oak floor which stretched to every room in her duplex. Her cell phone text message signal jangled in her bag. She dug through it until she reached the phone to read the message from Chip.

"U home"

"Yes. Just walked in."

"Be right there."

"K."

Maybe Chip would take her out tonight for a nice dinner and conversation. She had only talked to him briefly on the phone the day of the murder. He was out of town. Her heart lightened at the prospect of seeing him. Leaving the mail on the floor, she ran to the bathroom to primp a bit before he showed up.

A mixture of old and contemporary furniture graced the living room of her duplex, giving the open floor plan a shabby chic appearance. Lauren loved the mix of the contemporary black leather sofa with an afghan and the old rocking chair which used to belong to her beloved grandmother. She didn't even mind the over-sized upholstered gray recliner her dad insisted she take from the living quarters upstairs in the funeral home. It was comfortable after all.

A few throw rugs warmed up the room, adding splotches of color to the landlord beige walls. An old farm table with mixed wooden chairs graced the large window so Lauren had an unobstructed view of the countryside because only young trees were rooted by the road.

As she combed the snarls out of her thick, blonde hair, she heard the doorbell ring. Chip must've been down the street. She pulled through one more section of snarls, checked her make-up, straightened her light sweater, and dashed from the bedroom through the living room to let Chip inside.

When she opened the door, she almost giggled in delight when she saw he had a wrapped mixture of flowers from the grocery store. Who cared if they weren't from the florist? At least he thought of bringing flowers.

"Oh, Chip. Thank you." She launched herself into his arms. His big burly chest and his arms around her felt so good. She wiggled into the comfort of his embrace, feeling safe and protected by this man who maintained the strength he had when he was wrestling in high school. Her nose caught the familiar smell of cigarette smoke on his tee shirt, but she didn't care. No lovely citrus cologne or minty sweet breath when he kissed her on the lips. It was pure Chip.

"Hey, Babe, you okay?" He held her at arm's length, checking her from head to toe.

"I'm fine. Better now that you're here." She ran her fingers along his dark Vandyke beard. Arms wrapped around each other's waists, they stumbled through the entry way. Chip hugged her tightly to his side walking her into the kitchen.

The kitchen was separated from the living room by an upper counter top with seating for four bar stools, facing the built-in stove and cabinets on the kitchen side. The small kitchen had enough room for two to cook in the space, but that was about it. Sleek white cabinets and contemporary black ball-shaped pendulum lights lit up the counter area with recessed lighting in the cathedral ceiling throughout the open area. Lauren still didn't know which switch operated each of the banks of lights or which could be dimmed. She flipped them until the right ones popped on.

Opening the refrigerator, Chip peered in and grabbed a beer. "Hey, do you want one?"

He must be worried to offer her a beer. "No, no thanks. I'm good." She buried her nose in the lovely bunch of flowers, grabbed a paring knife from the drawer, and pulled a rose vase from under the sink. She filled it with warm water, chopped off the stems with the knife, and plunked the flowers into the vase. Immediately the room seemed brighter. She breathed in the delicious floral scent. Nice to smell them in her house and not on a casket.

Chip made his way to the recliner and dropped into it. "Tell me all about it. What'd you see? What happened? Poor Tony." He shook his head. "Do they know who did it?"

After she scooped up the flower stem ends and dropped them into the wastebasket under the sink, she moved to the couch.

Lauren related the story as best she could. Chip swigged his beer as she talked. He got up and grabbed another beer and returned to his seat. "They still have no idea who did it?"

"I haven't heard anything. The police are watching Dad's place, the nursing home, and my house until they find the killer."

Chip sat straight up out of the recliner. "Why are they doing that? They think you and your dad did it?" His face flushed red with anger.

"No, no, Chip. They're protecting us. Just in case..."

"Just in case someone is after you." He swore under his breath. "I think you should leave the area for a while. Go someplace where no one knows where you are."

Lauren was taken back by Chip's words. "Well, I guess we could, but nobody will bother us with the cops driving around twenty-four hours a day. Hey, let's forget about all of it and get a nice dinner. Okay?"

"You should leave as soon as possible. You let the cops catch the killer, then it'll be safe for you to return."

Chip drained the beer, set the can on the floor and got up. "Please, Lauren. At least think about it. Okay?"

"Well, I can bring it up to Dad and Randy. See what they say. But seriously, honey, the police are on the job. I see them around all the time." Her eyes softened as she grabbed his hands in hers. "Thanks for worrying about me." She stood on tip-toes and gently planted a kiss on his cheek.

"All right." Chip cleared his throat. "Let's go get something to eat. I'm starved."

* * *

The smoke from the campfire filled Lauren's nose making it hard for her to breathe. She had moved her lawn chair twice to get away from the smothering smoke, but maybe she was beginning to believe the old adage "smoke follows beauty." Yeah, she was a beauty all right.

Somehow the delightful, relaxing dinner with conversation had turned into a wiener roast at Chip's farm. They had no special reason for the occasion. His buddies were always getting together with kegs of beer, plenty of weed, and guy kinds of food like wings, ribs, brats, burgers, and of course, hot dogs.

The evening was a perfect summer night. The long Michigan days cast a light in the late evening that showcased the acres of rolling cornfields surrounding the DeYoung farm. The low sun in the sky would surely signal a huge round of spirited applause and shouting when the light sank into the small inland lake. The gang always cheered the sun on, as if their loud shouting and clapping would help the sun to set. Well, it was fun, she had to admit.

As she watched the western sky's blaze with the pinks and oranges of the sunset, Lauren took time this evening to count her blessings. Perhaps the events of the day and the gathering of old and new friends made her realize she had made the right choices in her life. Returning to her home town, being with her mom, helping her dad, and re-acquainting herself with old friends was not all bad.

"Hey, Sis," her brother Randy tapped her on her shoulder. She turned to see him with his side-kick Emmett standing nearby.

"Hey, Bro. How many hot dogs you had?" She grinned. She remembered his penchant for eating hot dogs ever since he was a kid. No one believed how many he could eat at one sitting…and still keep them down.

"Oh, hell, I lost count."

Emmett chimed in, "I think we lost count of beers too, didn't we?" He hung on to Randy's shoulders. Lauren noticed his slurred speech and the goofy look on his face. Emmett never said no to a beer.

"Do you think the cops are driving by here to keep an eye on us?" Randy asked.

"Oh, I don't know. We're here with friends. Don't worry. I'm sure we're safe. We aren't under-age drinking like in high school." She gave him a thumbs up signal.

The two strolled off to join another group of friends. Lauren stood up and stretched. She hadn't met some of the women at the party, so she decided to make the effort to join in the circle near the food table.

On her way around the campfire, Lauren spotted Chip on his phone and headed toward him. She approached him from the back and overheard his conversation.

"No, not now," he hissed into the phone. He shook his head. "No, I can't talk now. Let me call you back." He waited. "Okay."

"So who was that?" Lauren asked from behind him.

Chip whirled to face her. "Don't sneak up on me like that and eavesdrop on my conversations. Don't ever do that again." He shook his finger at her and stalked off.

Lauren winced. What was up with that? He had never talked to her with such disrespect. She wished she'd had a comeback, but she was so shocked, she couldn't think quickly enough.

Maybe the conversation was about business. It must be business. His dad, Al was transitioning into retirement, letting go of the everyday running of the farm. Chip was now in charge of the huge operation. Dairy cattle, crop management, managing the payroll, and paying bills. She had to give him a little slack since he had to juggle a lot of balls in the air at once. Being an only child, he had no other family to help him. Still, he had no reason to talk to her like that.

She joined him, standing with a group of friends around the fire. "Chip, I'm ready to go." Her tone of voice and scowl on her face should give him the message.

"Well, go ahead."

"I came with you, remember?" She faced him squarely with hands on her hips.

"Fine, give me a minute." He turned away, ignoring her.

She tapped him on the shoulder. "I have a big day tomorrow. I want to get home. If you don't want to give me a ride, I'll ask my brother," her voice flooded with anger.

Mentioning her brother seemed to get his attention. For sure, Chip wouldn't want to drag Randy into their argument. "Okay, okay." He twisted around to his friends who were watching the interaction. Pointing his thumb over his shoulder at Lauren, he said, "I gotta take the party pooper home. I'll be back though."

The group nodded and said good night. Lauren was relieved no one gave them a hard time about leaving early. Evidently their friends had heard enough to keep out of it.

Lauren and Chip walked back to his black truck parked on the side of the gravel road. They moved to their respective sides of the vehicle and got in. Chip slammed the door hard, jammed the key into the ignition, and stomped down on the pedal.

Lauren's head lurched backward as he spun tires on the loose gravel and launched into the roadway.

She watched Chip, looking for signs of intoxication. He wasn't drunk, but for some reason, he was mad at her.

"Hey, what did I do?" she asked.

"Nothing." He kept his eyes focused on the road ahead.

"Well, I certainly don't think…."

"Don't think. Don't think at all. My business is none of your business, okay?"

She wondered if something was wrong at the farm. Then she remembered Tony worked for Chip.

"I'm sorry about Tony. Really I am. I know he worked for you for a while. If that's what's bothering you, you can talk to me about it."

"I don't want to talk about it." His voice was so loud, she jumped. He kept his eyes on the road as they drove back to her place, exchanging no words between them.

Lauren hopped out of the truck and slammed the door. Chip mumbled "Good night," and drove off, leaving her standing on the sidewalk to her duplex.

She clenched her fists to her side. Men! She'd never understand their macho ways.

Chapter Seven

The morning sun should have cheered up Lauren, but it didn't seem to eliminate the darkness she felt this morning after the argument with Chip last night. He had seemed so distant lately. She wondered if there was another woman in the picture. After all, they had made an agreement not to tie each other down, no strings attached. Chip's malicious divorce from his ex-wife pretty much precluded him from making commitments to anyone. He was afraid to trust anyone again with his heart. Lauren didn't believe Chip was the soul mate for her for a lifetime. Partners for dinner and in the bedroom, but no commitment. It had worked for a couple of years, so far.

Lauren pulled her car into the nursing home parking lot and sat behind the wheel a minute to prepare herself for the visit with her mother. Ugly dread fell on her, as usual, never knowing how her mother would be or if she'd even recognize her. Guilt for not wanting to see her seeped into her soul. She didn't want any regrets after her mother was gone from this earth. She'd hang on to the good visits for her memories and discard the tough times forever. Taking a calming breath, she determined to handle whatever she might run into today, good or bad.

Lauren gathered the latest celebrity and home and garden magazines in her arms. Her mom could no longer read her books, her lifelong passion, but the colorful pictures in the publications usually coaxed out a smile.

"Good morning, Lauren." June, her mother's aide, greeted her at the nurse's desk with the big smile that lighted up her cocoa brown face and everyone who met her. This large woman had comforted Lauren more than once, enveloping her in a warm embrace after an especially difficult visit.

"Hello." Lauren tried to return a smile as big as June's, but found that nearly impossible to match. "How's Mom this morning?"

"Oh, Miss Barbara is up and ready this morning. She was gung-ho to get down to breakfast and ready to milk the cows until I told her they were way out on the farm." June shook her head. "She wasn't too happy about that."

Lauren nodded and smiled. "She was raised on a dairy farm and has told me stories a hundred times about her Holstein cow, Mabel. She won a lot of awards at the county fair." She winked at June.

"Well, I know you'll brighten her up, I'm sure, with all those magazines."

Lauren rolled her eyes. "I sure hope so."

June walked to the locked double doors preventing entry and exit from the Alzheimer's unit and punched in the code to open them.

"Have a good visit." Another smile spread across June's face.

Lauren took a deep breath. "Okay. We will. Thank you."

She walked down the sterile hallway of the Alzheimer's unit, broken up by doors to the residents' rooms and a few large paintings hanging on the green walls. Lauren greeted patients who stood in their doorways or sat in the wheelchairs in the hall. After nearly two years of visiting her mother, many of them had grown dear to her, but sadly some didn't even recognize her anymore and greeted her as a stranger.

Lauren pushed open the heavy door of her mom's room and walked in. The room was decorated with items brought from home, but even the familiar nick knacks, favorite dresser, and afghans didn't make it feel like "home."

Barbara stood at her dresser with drawers pulled out to the max, rummaging through the top drawer. Underwear, scarves, and night gowns lay scattered on the floor, the bed, and on nearly every surface possible in the small room.

"Hi, Mom," she said quietly not wanting to frighten her. "Can I help you? Are you cleaning out your dresser?"

"Oh, Lauren, they've taken my socks. I had warm socks, and now I'm missing several pairs. Those women have stolen my socks. You go down there and tell them I want them back." She threw her hands over her head, and quickly dropped balled fists to her sides. Her mother's eyes were filled with anger. June was right, she was not happy at all.

Lauren moved toward her anxious mother, noticing how her clothing hung on her thin frame. "Oh, Mom, I bet they're in the laundry hamper. Let's take a look." Lauren walked to the bathroom and opened the hamper going through the small amount of clothing. She pulled out two pairs of practically clean socks.

"Ta-dah!" She held up the socks proudly so her mom could see them.

Barbara did not smile. She stared at the socks, slammed the top drawer shut, and settled herself in her recliner.

"The lost is found," Lauren said as she tossed the socks back into the hamper.

"Not those socks, the ones I always wear with my navy blue slacks, you know with that flower design?" she said quietly, keeping her eyes on her hands clasped in her lap.

Lauren remembered the socks indeed, but they were ones her mother wore twenty years ago. Barbara fidgeted with her hands, a sign of her agitation.

"I brought you some magazines." Lauren pointed to where she had laid them on the small table by the door. She began picking up the clothing around the room and placing them in the dresser drawers. Her mother remained silent and withdrawn.

Lauren moved close to her mom and gave her a hug. Barbara didn't return the embrace but continued to rub her hands together.

"They're stealing from me. I know they are."

"Who's stealing from you? "

"Those damn nurses!" Barbara's outburst could have been heard all the way down the hallway. Lauren closed the door to the room and knelt by her mother.

"What's missing?"

"My socks. My socks are gone." She began to weep. "Somebody's taking my socks."

Lauren bit her lip. She never knew how to react to her mom's episodes. She took a calming breath and patted her mother's thin arm

"I need socks. They keep stealing them! You're going to have to take me out of here and buy me socks." Her mother's sad eyes locked into Lauren's.

"Okay, okay. We'll do that. We can get you some new socks." Lauren patted her mother's hands and held them so she wouldn't rub all the skin off of them. She pulled the frail hands to her lips and kissed them like her mother did with her when she was a little girl.

"Well, if your father were here, he wouldn't allow anyone to take my socks."

"He'll be here today. You'll see. I'll send some socks with him." Her dad never failed to visit her mother. He came every afternoon at dinner time to sit with her while she ate or at least tried to encourage her to eat. Lately Barbara had no appetite.

"No. No, he never comes to see me."

"Mom." She didn't want to argue with her. Arguing only spiked her irritation. There was no sense making her worse.

Lauren wished she could talk to her about the murdered man in the funeral home garage or ask her to help figure out why Chip was so mad at her. If only she could come back to reality. Unfortunately, she couldn't comprehend any of it.

Lauren spent an hour picking up the room and chattering to Barbara about the old days, but it didn't seem to help get her out of her pout about her missing socks.

"Those nurses are stealing my socks. I tell you, you cannot trust them."

She walked over to her mother again and put her arms around her. This time Barbara reached out and clung to her. It felt so good, so right. Lauren kissed her on the cheek and said, "I love you a million bushels full." It was a game they played when she was a girl and throughout her life. But this time her mother didn't reply with "I love you two million bushels full."

Lauren stepped back. Sadness squeezed her heart. Her mother looked so small sitting in that recliner. But that woman was not her mother, not the woman who raised her and loved her. She was a shell of the vibrant and caring woman who supported her unconditionally.

"I've got to go now." Lauren leaned over and gave her mom one more kiss, then whirled away from her to escape before her mother saw her tears.

Chapter Eight

"Ethel looks so much better now she's dead instead of when she was alive," Norma whispered to Lauren. "Well, you know what I mean. She was so sick at the end of her life." Lauren knew exactly what she meant. She had heard the statement many times at visitations.

"Your dad sure knows how to fix 'em up. I'm expecting him to do the same good job on me. Make me look 60 again, huh?" The white-haired woman's eyes sparkled with humor.

"You know, we'd do anything for you, Norma." Lauren responded with a wink.

Norma and her mother were best friends ever since she could remember. They met at church, and became very close when Norma began helping with funerals. After all these years, she still cleaned the funeral home and upstairs apartment where her father and brother lived. When the visitations were held at the funeral home, Norma was always ready to jump in and help to set up the flowers. Sometimes she and Lauren loaded them into the black van after the funeral and raced to the gravesite to set them around the grave opening before the family and friends arrived at the cemetery. She had a gift for arranging the pieces to soften the reality of the open grave. Norma's extraordinary care with all she did was her way of comforting the family.

Tonight Lauren was assigned to "swing door" for the visitation. Usually she, her dad, and Randy rotated the hours so someone could get a break. She was responsible for helping the grieving family with anything they might need and greeting those coming to pay their respects to the family of the deceased. The late-afternoon and into the evening duties involved setting up more chairs if needed, keeping up with the coffee, offering envelopes to those wishing to contribute to a memorial fund, and in general, being there for whatever people required of her.

The large front room, originally the parlor of the Victorian home, served as the visitation area and the chapel area for funeral services. Antique furniture, upholstered in creams and beige, carried out the theme of the Victorian era. Burgundy colored chairs and softly lighted lamps positioned along the walls of the room left the center open for friends and families to gather.

The recently departed reposed in the casket at the far end of the room with special lighting to add "life" to the loved one. Floral tributes placed artistically around the casket tempered the harshness of the scene. The family pieces were always displayed nearest their loved one. Most often the script explaining the relationship to the deceased was attached on a ribbon such as "aunt" or "mother."

The immediate family received hugs and messages of sympathy from visitors in the waiting line nearby. Others preferred not to stand by the casket and stood close to the entrance of the room in a receiving line much like the one following a wedding. In this case, smiles and joy were missing, replaced by hugs of sympathy and tears.

Lauren checked the room again. The number of mourners had dwindled to about half a dozen. They would stay until the final minutes of the visitation. She decided to take a break in the office. Her feet were killing her after standing all evening. Her morning had started early by visiting her mother. Plus she had put in a full day with office work, setting up the floral pieces, and getting ready for the visitation. She rolled her eyes, glad her job description didn't include embalming the body too.

She sat at her desk and pulled off the four-inch heels. Rubbing her sore feet, she vowed to put those high heels in the back of her closet. Even wearing them for a few hours was too long. But they were so cute. She frowned when she remembered how much she paid for all the torture.

"Oh, excuse me." A family member appeared in the doorway. "Sorry to bother you, but we're out of coffee."

Lauren managed to plaster on a pleasant smile when she saw the woman. "Oh thank you for letting me know. I can get another pot ready right now." Service with a smile. Her dad had drilled into her head they were to be there for the families, no matter what. "Put yourself in their place and treat them like you would want to be treated," he often repeated to her. She jammed her aching feet into her stylish, but painful, heels and hobbled to the family room.

After making yet another pot of coffee, Lauren returned to the chapel. As she strolled by the front windows, she spotted the police car driving slowly by the house. She had to admit the small town police force had kept their promise to patrol the area when the police were on duty from six in the morning till midnight. After midnight the county sheriff's deputies responded to calls in town. Lauren pushed her hair back from her forehead. Worry clouded her eyes when she realized the deputies had a lot of square miles in the county to patrol during the night.

She strained to see through the sheer curtains to get a glimpse of the driver. She hadn't seen Gary, but perhaps he was working a different shift. Disappointment shadowed her face.

After checking with the family about the arrangements for tomorrow's service, Lauren accompanied them to the door and said good-night. She closed the heavy oak door with inlaid bevel glass and locked it. She turned her back and leaned against it for a minute. Sighing with relief, she pulled off her shoes and wiggled her toes. How delightful.

A knock on the door jump-started her heart. She whirled around to discover a figure distorted by the beveled glass of the door. Could he be the killer? She hesitated to open the door.

"Hey, Lauren. It's me, Gary." Lauren recognized his muffled voice through the door and quickly unlocked it.

She smiled when she saw him. Gone were his Harry Potter glasses she remembered from high school and his brown eyes sparkled in the hallway light. Funny she'd never noticed his eyes before. Dressed in his police officer's uniform, he towered over her by at least six inches.

"Come on in. Oh my goodness, but you scared me," she exclaimed with her hand over her heart.

"Sorry. I thought you'd seen me walking up on the porch. Of course there was a crowd of people coming out of the house." He looked her over from head to toe. "Are you okay?"

"I'm fine. Glad you're here. Are you on official business?"

"Well, yeah, kind of. I thought I'd check the house inside. With the people attending the wake tonight, anyone could slip in and not be noticed."

Lauren's jaw dropped. "Are you serious? Someone could?" She put her hand over her mouth. "I never gave it a thought." She shivered as she imagined what could happen.

Gary reached for her shoulders and leaned down to face her. "I'm sorry if I frightened you, but we have to be honest and face the reality here. You and your family could be in danger." He gently squeezed her shoulders. "You're alone here now, huh?"

"Oh, sure, but I'm planning to lock up and get out of here. Been a long day."

"I see." He looked down at her bare feet. "Seems like the last time I saw you, you weren't wearing shoes." He grinned. "I think it would be a good idea to have someone here with you at all times. Seeing a single car parked out there is a giveaway that you're alone here. And we still haven't apprehended…".

Lauren held up her palm. "Okay, okay. I get the message. But I'm not some shrinking violet."

Gary's eyes narrowed, and he stepped away from her. "Of course you're not, but you have to take care of yourself. You don't need to prove how brave you are or offer any opportunity for someone to take advantage of a situation. You could be in extreme danger." "That's what I thought we had you guys for, to protect us." She folded her arms across her chest.

Locking his gaze on her, he said, "We can't always be in the right place at the right time. So don't give the bad guys any openings, okay?"

"Duly noted, Officer." She could hear the concern in his voice, and she liked it.

"Got time for a cup of coffee? I'll make some fresh while you check out the house."

"That sounds good. Let me take a look around."

"Great. I'll meet you in the family room. That's where the coffee pot is." He walked through the living room, checking for some creepy guy hiding behind the curtains she supposed.

Lauren hummed as she made yet another pot of coffee, but this time it was for her and Gary. She was looking forward to chatting with him and catching up.

As she measured the water into the carafe, the temperature in the room dropped, and she sneezed three times, a sure sign Henry was lurking nearby.

"Hi Henry." She never turned away from the counter. "Nice of you to wait till the family left for the evening. But Gary's here now. No need for you to stay around, right?" Lauren caught his shadow out of the corner of her eye.

"I guess you're right. Bad timing on my part. I don't want to interrupt your rendezvous with your old sweetheart." Henry bowed low, then stood and leaned on his umbrella.

Lauren chuckled as she faced Henry straight on. "Gary's not an old sweetheart. He was a good friend in high school though. We were very close especially since he could work out those trig problems for me."

"Oh, I guess I was mistaken. I thought you two were a couple."

"Say what?" She wrinkled her nose at the thought. She and Gary, a couple? She put her finger to her chin to think about that. Well, he does look pretty sharp in his uniform, broad shoulders, and those eyes. Somehow the nerdy boy with the big glasses and zitty face had evolved into a muscular cop.

Henry interrupted her thoughts. "How was your mother today?"

"About the same. Still confused. But she remembers me, Henry. I'm hanging on to that. She still remembers me, but she doesn't remember that Dad goes every day to visit her. I wonder if she doesn't know him."

"Oh, sorry, Lauren." Was that Gary's voice?

Lauren spun around to see him standing in the doorway. As he walked into the room, he said, "I heard you talking to someone, so I thought I'd better check in." He looked around and returned her gaze with questions in his eyes.

Her face flushed with embarrassment. "Oh, uh, no. Nobody's here. Just me talking to myself, I guess." She searched Gary's face to see if he bought it. Definitely a better explanation than telling him she was talking to a shadow.

"Come on in. The coffee should be ready in a minute." Lauren motioned Gary to have a seat on the couch in the family room.

"I'll be back after I check out the garage." Gary smiled. "I take it black."

"Oh, yeah, ok, the coffee." Her palm smacked her forehead with the knowledge Gary must have heard her talking to Henry. She glanced at the shadow and smiled back at him through clenched teeth.

Gary turned his back and headed down the hallway to the garage.

She felt as if Henry could see the steam escaping from her ears. She was so angry at that cocky shadow for staying to watch and see how she was going to explain her talking to him.

"Talking to yourself. That was good." Henry stood up straight. "You're pretty quick on your feet."

"Henry," she hissed in a hushed whisper. "Go away. I don't need you around here tonight. I have company,"

"I guess it's a bad time for us to have a talk now that Lover Boy is here."

Lauren bit her lip so she couldn't yell at the annoying Henry. She certainly didn't want Gary to hear her give that shadow a piece of her mind or he'd be back in a second with more questions.

Squeezing her eyes tightly closed, she said, "You'd better be gone when I open my eyes." Not that she could do anything if he didn't leave.

Lauren squinted through her right eye. Not seeing the shadow, she opened both eyes wide and swept the room and sighed with relief.

At that moment the basket full of sugar packets flew off the table onto the floor.

"Henry!" She couldn't stop herself from yelling his name out loud.

He didn't respond. He had slipped through the slice of time into another dimension

Chapter Nine

Ten minutes later, Gary stepped into the room. "I checked the house and garage. Looks like it's all clear here. Time for coffee?"

"Yes indeed. Have a seat." Thankfully, he didn't mention he'd heard her yell at Henry. She had picked up the sugar packets and wiped up the contents from a couple that had broken on the ceramic tile floor before Gary returned. She was glad she didn't have to make up another lie to explain why she was wiping up sugar.

Dreading the possibility Gary would bring up overhearing her talking to Henry, she tugged the hem of her tailored white blouse over her black skirt and took a cleansing breath to calm the swirling in her stomach.

Putting on her most angelic smile, she said, "It's decaf. I hope you don't mind. We only serve decaf. People are already overwrought with grief and nerves on edge when they're here. We don't want to add caffeine to elevate the situation."

Lauren turned away from the counter with a plain black mug in each hand. She watched Gary try to fit into the deep sofa and smiled as he sank into the cushions, and awkwardly moved forward to sit on the front of the seat with his elbows resting on his knees. When he saw her coming with the coffee, he stood up and grabbed one mug waiting until she sat at the other end of the sofa before he took his seat.

He faced her and raised his mug. "Cheers." They leaned toward each other and clinked the mugs together. As Lauren sipped the hot liquid, she watched Gary. He returned the look. She flipped her gaze down to her coffee mug. He blew across his mug to cool off the brew, and heat rushed into her face. It wasn't from the hot coffee.

"Been a long time," he said as he moved closer to her and rested the mug on his knee.

"Too long." The cushions of the sofa sank next to her

"Lauren." He gently touched her shoulder. Not taking his gaze from her, he said, "I know I'm late in saying it, but, I'm very sorry about Brandon." He tilted his head toward her. "I wanted to come to the funeral, but I was working in Utah and…" His voice splintered with emotion.

"Thanks. I'm doing a lot better now."

Brandon and Lauren had made wedding plans upon his return from duty in Afghanistan. But he never came home, not alive anyway. Although he had died more than six years ago, it seemed like it was yesterday. Gary's sincere comment touched a place in her heart filled with memories of Brandon.

She turned away from him to hide her tears. He placed his mug on the coffee table and gently hugged her. "I'm sorry. I shouldn't have said anything especially after all you've been through recently."

Lauren pulled away and noticed the sorrow in his face. "I don't know what happened to me. I can usually keep it together. Just thinking he was your friend too, I guess. We made quite a threesome in high school, didn't we?"

She flipped the tears from her eyes before they could flow down her cheeks. Gary pulled a tissue from the box on the coffee table and offered it to her.

Brandon, Gary, and Lauren grew up together, sharing great times and bad times. For too long she'd kept her emotions guarded from others so they wouldn't feel the pain of Brandon's loss or worry about her. But with Gary, it was different. She could share her emotions with him because he knew and understood her so well.

"Life isn't compartmentalized. I can't box up what Brandon and I had together and forget it. He's always with me tucked inside my heart. Sometimes I miss him so bad I don't think I can get through it. So I grieve again and wallow in self-pity for a time. Then I remember Brandon wouldn't want me to do that. So I pick myself up, and do something to get over it."

She dabbed her nose and eyes and squished the tissue in her fist. "I'm not a quitter. I won't let the grief beat me down."

"Hell, I know you're not a quitter." Gary's eyes brightened, and he squeezed her shoulder.

"Brandon was a special guy, a good friend. I miss him too. Damn good basketball player." Gary smiled. "Not so good in English though."

Time flew by as they shared memories of Brandon and the good old school days. They were so caught up in conversation neither touched their coffee even after it cooled off.

Finally taking a sip of her coffee, she asked, "So, what have you been doing for the last ten years?" She settled into the sofa, waiting for his answer.

"Well, I met a girl at college. Miranda. Fell really hard for her. We married and it lasted three years, all through college. When we graduated and entered the real world, our goals changed. I guess that's what you'd say. Her ideas of our future together and my ideas didn't mesh. So we ended the marriage amicably."

"Oh, Gary, I'm so sorry." She recalled some of the girls he dated in high school who she thought were not the best choices for him either. "Do you have children?"

"No, no. That was one of our deal breakers. She decided she wanted a career, not a family." He averted his gaze to his hands.

"Funny thing. We hadn't been divorced a year when she met another guy and married him. They have a baby now." He pulled himself up to sit on the edge of the couch.

"Well, she doesn't sound like the girl for you, for sure." She tapped his arm with her fingers.

"The divorce changed my life, my way of thinking" He inhaled deeply. "I thought I was going to do great research in medicine. Discover the cure for cancer or something that would help the world." His arms encompassed a make-believe world. "Instead, I changed the vision I had for my life. I still wanted to help people, so I decided to become a cop. I worked in a few cities, but being a small town boy, I hated living in the city. So I came back to Mayfield when there was an opening two months ago." He grinned at her, "And I'm very glad I did."

"I'm glad you did too." She squeezed his hand. "Do you have someone special in your life now?"

"No, I haven't found anyone...yet." His eyes darkened as he looked at her. "I hear you're hooked up with Chip. How's he doing?"

"Okay. His dad is giving him a lot more responsibility now on the farm, so he's busy." She didn't want to explain their relationship to Gary. In fact, she didn't even know if they still had a relationship.

"Hey, your coffee's getting cold. Let me get you a fresh cup." She reached for the mug, but Gary touched her hand and held it.

"Thanks, but I've got to get back on patrol. Really appreciate talking with you." He unfolded himself from the sofa and stood tall. "Next time, we'll have coffee someplace else rather than the funeral home, okay?"

She smiled. "Sure, any time."

"Why don't you gather your things and I'll walk you out to your car?"

"Oh, I'll be fine. I..." his serious face stopped her. He was back into his policeman role. No sense arguing with him. "Okay, Officer. Let me get my bag."

"Don't forget your shoes." She was delighted at his charming smile.

"Oh, yeah, I guess it's illegal to drive barefoot, eh?" She loved his teasing her like the high school days. Somehow, they had picked up where they left off ten years ago. She felt closer to Gary than she had ever believed possible.

She gathered her bag and phone from her desk and slipped on her shoes. He waited for her by the front door. Her heart skipped a bit, and she could feel herself smiling as she approached him. Why did she feel like she was sixteen again?

* * *

Following Lauren to her house that evening, Gary realized he was smiling. He couldn't remember the last time he smiled like this. Maybe he felt so good inside because he'd enjoyed reminiscing with Lauren about the teachers and classmates and catching up on the whereabouts of their friends from the "good old" high school days.

He shook his head and practically strangled the steering wheel when, like a bolt of lightning, he was struck at what made him happy tonight.

Lauren. Damn, there's that smile again. This time a low chuckle rumbled into the air.

The floral fragrance of Lauren this evening, her luscious curves, her bare feet. He grinned again remembering how comfortable it was to talk with her.

His brow creased with the thought of overhearing her talking with someone. Why did she try and cover it up? He definitely heard her talking out loud to someone. Then again when he stood in the doorway and looked to see who it was, no one was there. Was Lauren so stressed she was talking to herself?

Gary followed her when she turned left off the main road several blocks from her home. He'd been assigned to the detail to patrol her house and neighborhood when he was on duty. He probably drove by more often than the rest of the officers while on duty and even when not in uniform. The city needed more officers to cover this assignment, but a town this size didn't have the funds to pay a large force.

When they approached the house, his smile disappeared. He wanted to spend more time with her. She parked in the driveway and walked to her front door. He appreciated her soft curves observing her while she strutted to the door in her heels, not bare feet. As she unlocked it, she gave the thumbs up sign to him and dazzled him with her flirty smile.

Damn, she was beautiful. He beat the steering wheel with the heel of his hand. If only she wasn't involved with Chip. Chip, the spoiled kid when they were in school. Chip, the rich kid. Chip, the guy who was now running a huge million dollar plus farm. He didn't have a chance with Lauren.

His eyes opened wide with a realization. As if a lightning bolt had struck him, the idea that he wanted her crackled through his brain. When he was near her, the air sizzled. Did Lauren feel it too?

Chapter Ten

Lauren flipped on the light and kicked off her shoes when she walked into the entry way of her duplex. Gary had followed her home and waited till she gave him the thumbs up that all was well inside. Feeling a bit skittish that someone might be hiding in the garage, she had become accustomed to parking her car in the driveway. Her eyes shone brighter. Why hadn't she used the excuse of checking out the garage to invite him in? Another slap to the forehead.

Of course she was being silly, no one was looking for her. Still, she couldn't shake that underlying fear since the police hadn't arrested anyone for the murder.

Lauren was famished. She locked the door, grabbed her cell phone out of her bag, and made a bee-line for the refrigerator. Opening the door, she took inventory of the nearly empty appliance. Bagel, but no cream cheese, a couple of apples, beer, and milk.

When she grabbed the milk and set it on the counter, her phone signaled a text from Chip.

What? He couldn't even call her to apologize for his bad humor last night? She rolled her eyes as she clicked on the message.

"U home"

She typed in "yes."

"Be right there."

"K."

She stared at the message. She couldn't believe she agreed that he could come on over, when she really meant to say, "Yes, if you give me an apology for last night." Too late. At least this way he could apologize to her face-to-face.

Lauren grabbed a bowl from the kitchen cabinet and filled it with cereal and milk. As she slurped the last drop of milk from the bowl, someone knocked on the front door. She smoothed her hair and pulled the hem of her blouse over her skirt feeling butterfly wings fluttering in her stomach. Taking her time to reach the door, she unlocked it and stood in front of Chip.

"Gosh, it took you long enough to open the door," he growled and started to push past her.

Lauren stood her ground, blocking his way. "Just a minute, Chip." She glared at him. His expression of surprise indicated he had no clue why she was upset with him.

"What's goin' on? " He held his hands to his sides, palms up, as he stood on the front porch.

"I think you owe me an apology for the other night. You were rude and downright mean to me."

Chip shifted his weight from one foot to the other. Taking a deep breath, he said, "I'm sorry, Lauren. I had a rough day, and I guess I took it out on you." He squeezed her arms and pulled her to his chest for a hug.

She twisted away from him and gazed up into his eyes. Studying his contrite face, she said, "I'm sorry you'd had a bad day, but I sure didn't deserve that kind of treatment."

"What can I do to make it up to you?" He smiled. "Come on. Can I take you out for dinner?"

"I already ate."

"Well, how about you go out with me and keep me company? I'll buy you a drink."

"I got home. I'm tired."

"Hey, I told you I'm sorry. Really." She looked into those puppy dog eyes and the anger melted away. How does Chip always get his way? He always knew what to say to get what he wanted.

"All right, all right. I'll go with you. I guess I'll call that bowl of cereal an appetizer, not supper." She was disappointed for giving in so easily, but that cereal really hadn't filled her up.

"All right, I'll buy you a steak, a pizza, Mexican. Anything you want, baby." Chip gave her a hug. He stepped away from her. "Oh hey, can you drive? I'm about out of gas."

Lauren rolled her eyes. Well, at least he promised to buy her dinner. "Okay. I'll get my bag."

* * *

Chip and Lauren scooted into a back corner booth of the restaurant. The fake leather seat was so cold from the air conditioning, goose bumps popped up on her arms.

"I think they could turn down the air in here. It's freezing." Lauren said. She wished she hadn't changed to shorts and a tank top before they left her house. She rubbed her arms a bit, but that didn't help much with the blast of air aimed right at her.

"We can move to another table," Chip said. She looked around the nearly empty restaurant. She had her choice of many spots. Chip certainly was being thoughtful. Maybe her lecture on treating her right had sunk in.

"Okay. Let's move and make sure there's no AC duct blowing on us." She smiled at Chip. They found a booth far away from the kitchen making a longer walk for the waitress, but a tad bit warmer for her bare arms and legs. Besides, it was kind of nice to have the place to themselves.

"Order what you want, Lauren. How about a glass of wine with dinner?"

Lauren was taken aback by his solicitous attitude toward her. Was he feeling guilty about the way he disrespected her the other night?

"Thanks, but I've had a long day. If I have a glass of wine tonight, I'll be sound asleep before the main meal is served." She yawned. "See what I mean?"

Chip ordered the rib-eye steak and Lauren chose shrimp. It was pleasant to be sitting in the restaurant with a handsome man who was especially engaging with his stories.

"Have they got any suspects yet for Tony's murder?" Chip reached into the basket for another dinner roll and slathered it with butter.

"It's only been a few days, but I haven't heard a thing from the police. They've questioned the neighbors. Thankfully the tape is down and we can use the garage again. Dad made a removal yesterday and was able to drive in and unload."

"A removal?" His brow furrowed.

"Yeah, you know. When we pick up the body and bring it to the funeral home? One time when Dad went to pick up an old man at his home, he asked where was the deceased and his wife said, 'sitting in his favorite chair.' Dad just thought the old guy in the chair was asleep." She grinned and he chuckled. It felt good to be with this pleasant side of Chip.

The waitress brought the tray of food to the table. Lauren's stomach clenched with hunger when she smelled the smoky steak and the fried shrimp. She grabbed her napkin and smoothed it across her lap as the waitress placed the dish before her so she could be ready for her first bite immediately.

The waitress stepped back and glanced at the couple. "Do you need anything else?"

With her fork in midair, Lauren shook her head no.

"No, I think we're all set and ready to eat," Chip said. "Thanks."

After the first bite of shrimp, Lauren took the time to relish the taste of the next bite. Good food, good guy, great evening. She relaxed for the first time in several days and felt peace.

Chip broke her reverie with his question. "Still have the cops watching your place and the funeral home?" He took an enormous bite of the buttered roll.

"Oh, yeah. In fact I talked with Gary for quite a while this evening. He was on duty and checked the house for me. As if he's going to find any bad guys hiding in the funeral home." She wrinkled her brow and shook her head. "Most folks don't like to come to our place, well, I guess, unless they're dead."

"I'm sorry you had to go through all of this and live with the aftermath of it." Reaching across the table, he placed his large hand over Lauren's. She felt the warmth of this gesture and felt all fuzzy inside with his caring about her.

"Chip, don't be concerned about me. I'm thinking about Dad. This incident is worrying him to death. Well, not literally to death. But he can't sleep or eat. He's like a man on a mission determined to keep us all safe. He's even worried someone will go after mom in the nursing home. I don't know how to handle it. Randy's no help." She placed her other hand on top of Chip's. "Thanks so much for caring about me." Lauren felt much better after spewing her worries to Chip.

After enjoying the meal and conversation, Chip said, "Okay, I guess we'd better get out of here before they lock us in." He grabbed the check and opened his billfold to pull out some cash. After rifling through the bill compartment, he chose a credit card and put it in the folder with the bill. A few minutes later, the waitress came by and took it to the front of the restaurant.

In a few minutes, she returned. "Sorry, but your card was rejected, sir."

"What?" He grabbed the credit card and checked it out. "Here." He put it in his wallet and pulled out another card. "I guess I gave you the wrong one." He laughed.

When the waitress walked away, Chip said, "Kind of tough being a farmer this time of year. No income till the crops come in this fall."

"Yep, bad as a funeral director in between funerals. There's never a guaranteed pay day." Lauren grinned.

"Last year, the crops didn't produce so good, so I'm a bit short on cash this year. You know the crops are growing great in the field, but Lauren, seriously." He hesitated for a minute, and then licked his lips. "Do you have any cash you could loan me till we sell the crop?"

Her eyes searched his face. "Are you serious, Chip? Are you asking me to float you a loan?"

He lowered his gaze to the table. Picking up the glass, he said, "Well, if you could consider it." He put the glass to his lips and looked over it at Lauren as he took a big gulp of water.

He was asking her for money and his dad had the biggest farm in the county.

"Well you know I'm good for it. I'll pay you back every penny this fall." There were those puppy dog eyes again.

"Hey, I know your dad's credit is good at the bank…"

Chip interrupted her. "I'm in charge of the farm now. I don't want Dad to be involved in this." He set the glass down hard on the table.

"Well, how much do you need?"

"I could use $10,000."

Lauren sat straight up, her hand to her chest, and couldn't stop the gasp escaping from her throat. He was asking her for $10,000? "You're out of your mind. I don't have that kind of money."

"Well, how about five thousand?"

"Okay, now I know you're joking." She glared at him. "It's a joke, right?"

"No, no joke." He took her hand. "I could really use five thousand dollars. If you don't have it, I'm sure your dad would give it to you. Of course, I wouldn't want you to tell him the money's for me." She jerked her hand away from him.

"So this is why you brought me out here and wined and dined me? To soften me up to ask for a loan?" The anger exploded into a hot red flush on her face and neck.

"That's absurd, Chip. I don't have that kind of money to give you. And for you to think I would ask my dad? That's ridiculous. Forget it!"

She scooted out of the booth and stomped toward the door. She couldn't even discuss the idea with Chip anymore. He was playing her for a fool, and she had figured him out after all.

She pushed through the doors of the restaurant, unlocked her car door and slid in. Shoving her key into the ignition, she slammed the door. When Chip came through the doors, she rolled down her window and yelled, "You'll have to find your own way home. I'm so angry; I can't even talk to you!"

Chapter Eleven

The next morning, Lauren greeted the grieving family as they entered the foyer. Her quarrel with Chip last night seemed insignificant when compared to the loss of their teen-age son, brother, nephew in a car accident. What words could she offer to comfort them?

The teen, Jason, and his friends attended a party hosted by a teen whose parents were out of town. Reports indicated the kids partied with alcohol and marijuana. The driver lost control of the car and crashed into a tree. Jason was killed, one boy was in critical condition, and the driver and another passenger were injured, but would mend physically. It would take a lot longer for them to recover emotionally from the experience, scarring their futures forever with memories of that deadly night.

Lauren couldn't help but wonder why Jason and his friends weren't stopped by someone at the party who would have noticed they were in no shape to drive. No one should have let them leave the party in that condition.

"Good morning, I'm Lauren Staab. My sympathy to you and your family." When Lauren offered her hand, she gazed into the mother's sorrowful eyes. A chunk of her heart broke off.

"Please come this way." Lauren was relieved to be able to walk the woman, her sister, and Jason's older brother to the family room where Lauren's father waited. After forty years in the funeral business, she was proud of her dad's gift to shepherd families through this most heart wrenching time. His understanding and caring helped families to deal with the devastating reality of their loss.

She offered coffee and beverages. They politely refused them. Lauren wished she could offer them something that would replace their deep sorrow and loss. She hated it when people said time will take care of the grief. That is no comfort to folks who are struggling to get through one hour, even one day, knowing they will never see their loved one again.

* * *

After meeting Jason's family, her thoughts focused on her friend, Stephanie, and how she was going to get through her life without her fiancé, Tony.

Settling into her office chair, Lauren stared at the monitor without actually seeing it. She rested her elbows on her desk and held her head

At Tony's funeral a few days earlier, Stephanie's tears flowed down her face during parts of the service. Lauren hugged her and stayed close to her and her family. His death was still so raw, there could be no comfort for Stephanie and the family and friends gathered there on that day.

Lauren shuddered when the memory of Tony's funeral morphed into the image of his body sprawled on the floor of the garage. She straightened up in her chair and pushed her hair back from her face. She couldn't bring back Tony for Stephanie, but she could do her best to find out who murdered him. She arched an eyebrow and tapped her finger to her chin. She could try and squeeze Gary for information. Maybe with his help she could put the puzzle pieces together to lead them to the killer.

Sneaking a cigarette and lighter out of her desk drawer, she decided maybe one smoke would help clear her head of the images of the murder and her heartbroken friend, Stephanie. When she walked out the back door of the funeral home, she noticed Emmett's truck parked in the driveway. She heard angry voices echoing in the garage.

Lauren entered the back door of the garage and spotted Randy and Emmett in a heated conversation. When they saw her, they immediately shut up.

Closing the door behind her, she walked up to them and said in a hushed voice, "Gosh, guys, keep it down. Dad's meeting with a family inside. Take your little quarrel somewhere else."

Emmett smiled so big, she wanted to slap his flushed face. He stumbled toward her and rested his hand on her shoulder. "Oh, Lauren. Nice of you to come by."

She noticed his red, blood-shot eyes and smelled his sewer breath. He was high.

Keeping her gaze on him, she said, "What are you guys doing out here?"

"Emmett was just leaving, weren't you, Emmett?" She swung her gaze to her brother. Randy placed his palms on Emmett's back and shoved him toward the door.

"Wait a minute. Wait a minute. You owe me, Randy. I'm not leaving till you pay me." Emmett shook his finger at her brother.

"Go home, Emmett. Get outta here." Randy raised his voice.

Lauren shushed him. "Hey. I told you there's a family in there."

Randy pulled his wallet from his back pocket and opened it. "Here's twenty bucks. I'll get the rest of the money when I go to the ATM, okay?"

Emmett snatched the twenty dollar bill from his hand. He circled his finger and thumb and looked through the circle with one squinted eye. "Okay, brother. We're friends. I'll trust you for it."

"I can trust him for it, can't I, Lauren?" He raised his chin and winked. "We've been friends too long to let a little weed break us up, huh?"

Lauren's eyes widened. "Don't tell me. You guys gotta be crazy. There are cops watching this place. You know that!"

"Oh, I've got plenty for them if they want it." Emmett laughed like a mad man. "I've got more stashed in the truck. Maybe I should go ask 'em?"

"You're disgusting, Emmett. Go take your business someplace else. Like Hell." Her arm slashed the air like a sword as she pointed to the door. She realized she had increased her voice a few decibels, then shut down, hoping no one heard her.

The lights in the garage flicked on and off; the automatic garage door squealed on its tracks up toward the garage rafters. Oil cans, cleaning supplies, and paper towels flew off the shelves.

The three jumped away from the flying debris.

"Hey. Hey, what're you doing?" Emmett looked wide-eyed at Randy and Lauren. "I'm gettin' out of here. This place is crazy!" Dodging the flying objects, Emmett beat it through the door to the safety of his truck. The vehicle's spinning wheels tossed the gravel against the garage as he roared off.

Randy and Lauren turned in circles checking the now quiet, but disastrous mess strewn throughout the garage. They faced each other.

"What did happen here?" Randy spread his hands palms up.

"I was going to ask you that, big bro. How'd you do that?" Lauren couldn't help but bust out laughing at Randy's puzzled look. Lauren knew, but she could never explain to her brother that Henry, her favorite shadow person, was riled up and showed it.

As she recalled the conversation with Emmett, the heat of anger flooded up her neck and into her cheeks. "Seriously, Randy. Were you buying weed from Emmett?"

"Let's just say, I did buy some from him and owed him for it. He must've needed some cash 'cause that was a long time ago."

"You're crazy to smoke that stuff." She crossed her arms across her chest and straightened her spine. "To think you're out here in the garage paying off a debt for marijuana." Her voice choked out the rest of the words. "While a family inside is making funeral arrangements for their dead son who died because he and his friends were partying with weed." She wanted to shake some sense into him.

"Well that has nothing to do with me." He pointed to his chest. "I didn't sell it to him."

"It has everything to do with you. Emmett, your friend, could be selling it to those kids. And you keep him in business buying from him."

Randy leaned forward into Lauren's face. "Hell no. He wouldn't do that. Are you crazy? You know him better than that."

"Do I?" She turned her back to him and pitched the unlighted cigarette on the floor. "Emmett's changed. He isn't the guy you knew when you were friends in high school. I think you need to help him realize drugs are taking over his life." Lauren waited a minute for a response from Randy, but all he did was shrug and begin to pick up the debris on the garage floor.

"I'm serious. Get him off drugs. Make him stop selling them." She accented each word with pumping fists.

Randy stood with hands holding oil cans and rags. "You're seeing things that aren't there. He's fine. Drop it!" Lauren saw the anger color his face.

"Don't yell at me for pointing out the truth. I know you can see it. Why can't you admit it?"

"Forget it, Lauren. Emmett's behavior is none of your business and none of mine either." He turned his back to her.

"You'd better pay better attention to him and help your friend. He's going to need help or it will be too late for him."

Randy whirled around to face her. "Shut up and help me pick up this mess."

"I've got things to do in the office. Get your friend Emmett to help you clean it up." Lauren strode out of the garage without looking back.

Chapter Twelve

Lauren entered her office and slammed the door behind her. She was infuriated with her brother and Emmett. She stomped to her desk and tossed the cigarette lighter in the drawer. The heat of her anger still flamed inside her.

"Lauren, you really should give up smoking those cigarettes. They can kill you." Her eyes darted toward the dark shadow next to the closed door. Once again Henry showed up at the wrong time. *But, when was the right time to see a ghost?*

Stifling the three little sneezes that always signaled Henry's presence, she said, "Oh, please, Henry. You aren't exactly a healthy specimen yourself, a smoky shadow. Are you telling me cigarettes killed you?" She smirked at him.

"No, not cigarettes."

"I think you know this isn't the right time to be discussing my health. That was you knocking the stuff off the shelves and flashing the lights on and off, wasn't it?" She practically stared a hole through the shadow.

"Why, what do you mean, dear?" It's a good thing Henry didn't have a face to slap because she would have if she could.

"You know what I mean." She sighed. "I guess I should be grateful instead of mad at you. At least your shenanigans scared off Emmett.

"You're welcome." Henry bowed deeply. "Glad to be of help."

Lauren sat down in her desk chair. "I don't know what to do about Emmett. Selling weed. I mean really. I always thought it was harmless fun when we smoked it around the campfire. But teenagers are using it. Who knows, it might filter down to the younger kids." She put her head in her hands. She recalled the sorrow in the eyes of the mother who was at this moment making funeral arrangements for her sixteen-year-old son.

She raised her gaze and spoke directly to the shadow. "I could report him to the police, but so what? I'd probably get Randy and my friends in trouble for buying the stuff." She shook her head. So many repercussions if she mentioned anything about Emmett and his drug deals. She slumped in her chair.

For once, Henry didn't have a word to say.

. "Well, I've got work to do, Henry." Tapping her computer to wake it from its hibernation, she said, "By the way, what did kill you?" Funny how she'd never even thought about how Henry died.

"Some bad guys didn't like me too much." He twirled his umbrella and tucked it under his arm.

Now that statement spiked Lauren's curiosity. "Do you mean somebody murdered you?" Her eyes grew wide with the realization. "Why? Were you a bad guy or a good guy?"

She heard Henry's deep chuckle. "Now how am I supposed to answer that? Of course, I think I'm the good guy." He gave the "thumbs up" gesture to emphasize he truly was.

Lauren leaned forward in her chair. She waited. "Well aren't you going to tell me what happened?"

A knock at the office door interrupted the conversation.

"Looks like I'd better leave now. I'm sure you don't want me hanging around when Lover Boy shows up."

"Lover Boy? You mean Gary?" She smiled at the thought of seeing him again. Henry nodded, then vanished.

Henry's term for Gary was funny but could Gary ever be her "Lover Boy?" Dang, she could feel that goofy smile spreading across her face again.

Lauren called, "Come on in, Gary."

Gary, dressed in his police uniform, opened the door wide. He looked up and down the hallway before stepping into the office and peering behind the door. "How'd you know it was me?" he asked with a puzzled look on his face.

Lauren's smile faded. *A shadow told me. No, that's probably not the right answer.*

Ignoring his question she said, "Well, hey, come on in. Good to see you." She plastered a big grin across her face as she stood and walked toward him. "What brings you here? Have a seat." She motioned to the chair in front of her desk.

"Thanks, Lauren, but this isn't a social call." He straightened his shoulders.

She stopped and searched his face. "What do you mean? Why are you here?"

"Detective Richards wants to talk to you. I'm here to escort you to the police station." His face was so serious, she thought perhaps he was trying to play a joke on her.

"Really? More questions about Tony's murder?" Gary didn't offer an answer.

"Gosh, he could give me a call. Or at least give me an appointment. I'm right in the middle of---"

Gary interrupted her. "No, Lauren. He's ready to talk to you as soon as we get there. Get your purse. We're leaving right now. I'll bring you back after." His commanding voice startled her.

Lauren couldn't believe this was the nerdy kid with the pimples she remembered from high school. Gary had grown up into an attractive man with broad shoulders and muscled arms and with a powerful presence she liked.

"Okay." She took her purse from the drawer. "I'll do anything I can to help catch the murderer."

Chapter Thirteen

The police station along with the city offices and chamber meeting room were housed in a new flat-roofed brick building. The few jail cells were located in the basement. The short drive to the station was very quiet with stoical Gary. Lauren wasn't sure if she could talk to him about the case or even the weather. He must be wearing his policeman hat today, not his friend cap, she thought.

Not waiting for Gary to open the car door for her, she exited the cruiser and caught a glimpse of a gaggle of local people watching her. She could feel their eyes on her as she made her way down the long sidewalk from the parking lot to the back door of the building. A couple waved to her, but most turned to comment to each other. She felt as if she were traveling down the walk of shame, and wanted to scream at the bystanders that she wasn't guilty of anything. She was there to help with the investigation not to be arrested for anything. She hoped.

The hallway leading to the headquarters was clean and brightly illuminated by the latest in lighting fixtures for contemporary buildings. The smell of the new paint wafted through the bland vanilla-colored hall to the police station entry door.

"Hi, Lauren." The young woman at the desk greeted her with a big smile. Her face was familiar to Lauren, but she couldn't place her.

"Hello, how are you?" Lauren had finally learned to add the "how are you" when she didn't know the person's name.

"Gary, you can go on in to Detective Richards office. He's waiting for you."

"Okay, thanks, Deb." Lauren tucked Deb's name into her brain so the next time she could call her by name. What was she thinking? She hoped there wasn't a next time to visit the police station.

Her palms were sweaty and she wondered if she had applied any deodorant this morning. Was she nervous because she was meeting the gorgeous detective or because she didn't want to relive the morning she saw Tony sprawled on the floor of the garage? Perhaps there was a flicker in her brain that the police were calling her in here to arrest her for the murder. She shook her head. No way could that happen.

When they walked in, Detective Richards stood to greet them from behind his desk. "Good morning, Miss Staab. Come in and have a seat. Officer Applegate, please stay." The dazzling blue eyes were as breathtaking as Lauren remembered. The rugged chin and broad chest under his white shirt and tie re–affirmed his stature as someone she'd like to get to know.

She glanced about the small office with a filing cabinet, a neat desk with a monitor, and a few framed awards and photos. She frowned. Several family photos of the detective and his wife and two young children were placed on a corner of a table that held the copy machine.

As she took a seat in the wooden chair across from the detective, he said, "Thank you for coming over." He waited until she was seated, then smoothed his tie as he settled into his extra large desk chair. "As you know we're investigating the murder of Anthony VanZant. "His eyes looked right through her. Definitely no small talk. He was getting right down to business.

"We've been following up all the leads we have, but so far, nothing substantial has surfaced that will answer the question as to why Mr. VanZant was killed and left in the funeral home garage. We're missing a link. What is it, Miss Staab?" The detective placed his elbows on the table and leaned toward her.

Lauren squirmed in her chair under his intense scrutiny. His question caught her off-guard. She looked up at Gary who was casually balanced, half sitting, half standing, at the copy machine table. He couldn't help her.

"Well, what can I say? I'm as much in the dark as you are, sir." She bit her lip.

"How do you know Mr. VanZant?"

"He is, was engaged to my good friend, Stephanie. We hung out a lot together. I was going to be in their wedding." Her voice choked. She squeezed her hands together in her lap while she marshaled her emotions. "Piper, Stephanie, and I were like the three musketeers in high school. We're very close."

"Did someone have a grudge against Tony?" He waited for her answer. Lauren's mind whirled with images of Tony laughing at their dumb jokes, getting her a beer at their home, opening doors for her.

The detective interrupted her thoughts. "Do you know of anyone in his past or present who would be so angry with him they would take his life?"

Lauren shook her head. "Oh, no. Tony was the sweetest guy. Everyone loved him."

"What is it? What aren't you telling me?" His eyes locked with hers. She felt like a bug under the detective's microscope.

Clearing her throat, she said, "Tony's ex-wife, Leah, is not always happy with him, but she certainly wouldn't kill him to get full custody of their eight-year-old son."

"Tell me more about that."

"Well, it's just that she…" Lauren felt like she was tattling on Leah. They had all gone to school together. But they weren't kids anymore. "Leah has a problem with drugs and alcohol. Let's say sometimes their son is not taken care of because she has that problem." Lauren pulled a strand of hair behind her ear.

"Let me be very honest with you. We're looking at why his body was dropped at the funeral home. What is the connection for this man to be found there instead of out in the woods or even disposed of in the river? Someone is trying to tell you something."

Lauren sat straight up in her chair. "Tell me something? Tony was killed because of me?"

"Well, perhaps because of you, your father, your brother. We don't know. We're trying to get to the bottom of this. Anything you can tell us could help lead us to the murderer."

Lauren's eyes widened. "Are you saying that my father, brother, or I have something to do with Tony's murder?" Lauren shuddered. She couldn't breathe.

* * *

Gary stood back and observed the scene. Lauren took several deep breaths to collect herself as she sat in the chair in front of Detective Richards. Gary wanted to get in the detective's face and say, "Stop it. Lauren has nothing do with this murder. Quit badgering her." But speaking to Richards like that would get him thrown out of the room and written up in his files. Neither would help Lauren.

Instead he studied her as she straightened her shoulders in the chair preparing to answer the detective. He recalled that determined look on her face before several incidents that occurred on the playground when they were kids. She could beat up any boy who hassled her and make him cry. She had her jaw set. He nodded. She could handle herself, and Detective Richards, just fine.

"I have no idea what you're waiting for me to say. I resent that you're implicating my family and me in Tony's murder." She didn't lower her gaze from the detective's eyes, drilling through her.

Gary quietly delighted in seeing the feisty girl he remembered come through.

Moving to the front of the chair and leaning toward the detective, she said, "I'm done here. I know nothing more about the incident or anyone connected to it. And that's the truth."

"Miss. Staab, you have to face the fact, Mr. VanZant was dumped at the funeral home for a reason." His gaze didn't waiver. "The sooner we figure that out, the sooner you and your family will be safe." He pushed his chair back from the desk and stood.

"Am I under arrest?" Her voice was tinged with anger.

"No, but if you do remember…"

Lauren picked up her bag and marched out of the office. Gary slid off the corner of the copy table and moved to the doorway of Richards' office, keeping her in sight as she strode to the back entrance of the building.

"Take her home. Let her stew a bit about the idea of her family's involvement in this case. If she finally gets it that they're all in danger, she may give us information that she doesn't realize is important in the investigation." He dropped back down in his chair.

"Yeah. Thanks a lot for letting me take her home. She's not too happy with you, but I'm the one who's going to get the brunt of it after your questioning her. Not looking forward to this drive." Gary shook his head in dismay and headed out to face the wrath of Lauren.

* * *

"I don't get it. What does Richards want me to tell him? " Sitting in the passenger seat of the cruiser, Lauren wrestled around in her bag trying to find her pack of cigarettes.

"And why didn't you stand up for me? Why'd you just sit there so placidly? I mean, really! I thought we were friends. Old friends." She shook out the last cigarette from the recovered pack.

"Sorry, Lauren, You can't smoke in this police car." He quickly turned his gaze back from her unlighted cigarette to the road ahead, but he could feel her angry glare on his cheek.

"I can't really discuss anything that went on in there with your interview."

"So that's it? That's all you're going to say to me after I was humiliated in that office?" She took the unlighted cigarette out of her mouth and waved it in the air at him when he dared to look back at her angry face. The only good thing to come out of her state of agitation was her eyes were bluer than he'd ever seen.

"I was hoping we could team up together so we could figure out who killed Tony. But you don't even want to discuss it with me?" She foraged in her bag for something else.

"It's not that I don't want to help, but you've got to understand…."

"Oh, I understand all right." She pulled out her cigarette lighter and shook it at him. "My friend, the person I have always trusted, won't help me find a murderer and prove me and my family innocent." Her voice cracked.

Gary glanced back at her. She was staring down at the opened bag on her lap and wiping her eyes with the back of her hands still clenching the cigarette and lighter.

The knot in his throat kept him from saying anything, but the ache in his chest for her made him pull the cruiser into a deserted alley and cut the engine.

"I'm sorry, Lauren." She wouldn't face him. "Hey, Lauren." He unbuckled his seat belt and placed his hand on her shoulder. She didn't flinch away but instead allowed him to rub her shoulder gently. He caught her gaze when she looked at him with her beautiful face twisted in anguish. He wanted to slide over and hug her to him. But would she hug him back?

"The best thing I can do is to do my job." She started to speak, but he held up his hand to stop her. "I'm determined to find Tony's killer too, but I care too much for you to involve you in this case. We're dealing with a dangerous person or persons." He brushed her hair from her face and didn't move his hands away from the smooth strands.

Gary steeled himself against getting lost in her blazing blue eyes. "I would give anything not to have you and your dad find Tony's body in the garage. But the fact is, you did. So now, the police are trying to track down all possible motives to find a suspect. You've got to let us do our job." He reluctantly pulled his hands away from her hair, but stayed close to her inhaling her lavender-scented fragrance.

"You don't need to take it so personally. Richards is doing his job, maybe not handling it so well in your case, but he's a good detective. He'll figure it out, but he needs all the information he can get to do that."

"Well, wouldn't you take it personally if someone accused you of murdering Tony?" Her eyes flashed with anger.

"I think the detective came off pretty hard-hearted with you. Like I said, he's trying to dig in and find out everything." Her expression seemed to soften.

Lauren threw her cigarette and lighter in her bag. "Okay. I get it."

"Good." He reached behind him for his seat belt and clicked it closed.

"Do you really care about me, Gary?" Her soft voice touched his heart.

His throat felt like it was clogged with cotton balls. Taking a deep breath, he turned to her and said, "Of course I do. I care about you very much."

Gary turned on the ignition and wanted to pound the steering wheel. *Stupid, stupid, stupid. Why didn't I tell her I loved her and have always loved her?*

Chapter Fourteen

That evening Lauren was content to sit in her car in her driveway and wait for a break in the rain. The sound of the rain spattering on the roof calmed her. Besides, she didn't have the strength to get out.

Thoughts of Gary flooded her mind. Sitting so close to him in the cruiser this afternoon immersed in his world of police work, the smell of the leather seats, the myriad of equipment in the cruiser, was a turn-on for her. Or was it his eyes, the muscles concealed under the uniform, or that moment of electricity that flashed through her when he said he cared about her?

Maybe she imagined it. Did she misread his feelings for her? Just like imagining Henry was in her mother's room at the nursing home this evening. She thought she felt his presence. Because she was so worried about her mother, maybe her mind zoned out for a minute.

After visiting her mom, she felt as limp as her old stuffed Raggedy Anne doll. The strong, vibrant mother she remembered was absent. The woman whose sparkly eyes danced with mischief when she played a prank on her unsuspecting family members was lost.

She replaced the image of her mother's thin form lying in the bed tonight, weakened by a fever, with thoughts of her mother as the healthy prankster. Lauren smiled when she recalled the April Fool's joke her mom pulled by moving all the clocks in the house up one hour. What a chaotic morning when Lauren and Randy were scrambling to get to school on time. They drove in to the high school parking lot to discover no one was there.

Her face crumpled at the reality of her mother's deteriorating quality of life. She rested her forehead on the steering wheel believing even the heavens were shedding tears with her as she struggled with loss, sadness, frustration. In the safe surroundings of the interior of her car, Lauren let her tears fall from her eyes, trace down to her chin, and drop onto the steering wheel. Her shoulders shook with sobs of grief and loss.

The burden was growing every day and finally, she could no longer pretend that everything was going to be fine. Her mom was never again going to be the mother who raised her. She was consumed by the darkness of the disease. It was only going to get worse for her mom.

Lauren gasped for breath. Her lungs were shrinking and her body trembling. She sat up straight in the driver's seat, breathed deeply, and grabbed a tissue from her bag to wipe the tears from her eyes and dab her nose. Lord she needed help. They all needed help. She breathed a ragged sigh.

Determined to face the future head on, she took a few more minutes to sit in her car with the quiet rain soothing her broken spirit. She wadded up the damp tissue and placed it in the litter bag in the pocket of the door. When she reached for her bag in the front passenger seat, her cell phone played a familiar ring tone. She knew from the heavy metal guitar sound, it was Chip.

Ignoring it, she opened the door, but quickly pulled it closed. He wasn't texting. He was actually calling her.

Wondering why Chip was calling, she dug into her bag, found the phone, and answered. "Hi, Chip. I just got home and I don't feel like talking. I'm exhausted."

"Lauren, I need help." His voice was only a whisper.

Lauren's hairs on her neck stood upright. "What's wrong? Where are you?"

"I drove my car off in a ditch. Can you come and get me?"

"Are you hurt? Want me to call 9-1-1?"

"No, no," he practically spat out the answer. "Don't call anybody. Come and get me. I'm on Warner north of the bridge that crosses Jenkins Creek. Hurry, will ya'?"

The urgency in his voice scared Lauren. "Okay, I'm in the car. I'll be there in a few minutes. Do you want me to stay on the phone with you?" Only silence was on the other end of the phone call. Was he dead?

* * *

Lauren raced down the city streets and out into the countryside oblivious of the rain-slickened roads. Warner Road was a black-topped two lane road used as a shortcut to Grand Rapids. Thank goodness this time of night no commuters clogged the roadway.

The moonlight filtered through the moving clouds not offering much light for her to see Chip's car. She turned on her bright lights hoping he would see her and wave her down. That is, if he could walk up to the road. The ditch was deep, and rugged country bordered the roadway.

The headlights flashed on movement ahead. She could only see his head and hand waving from the ditch. She braked quickly and pulled over to the right shoulder of the road. He pulled himself up to the car before she could stop completely. He was bent over like a crooked old man. Chip opened the door and eased in.

When she saw his face from the car's ceiling light, her stomach turned over. Blood soaked the handkerchief he held to his forehead and rivulets of red traced his cheeks and down his arm. He groaned as he pulled the door shut and slumped over cradling his chest.

Lauren's heart pounded in her throat. Was he going to die right here in her car?

She looked through the car windows for Chip's vehicle. "Where's your truck?"

"It's down there in those trees."

She strained her eyes, but couldn't see anything in the darkness.

"Hurry up. Get outta here," he yelled at her.

"Okay, I'll take you to the hospital." She made a U-turn on the road and slammed her foot on the accelerator wishing she had a siren and red light so she could speed. Now when she wanted the police to be watching over her, there was no one in sight.

"No, no hospital. Take me to your house. I can't go to the hospital." He bent his body further over as if hiding in the car.

"So you were driving drunk. Is that it? Do you want a DUI?" Why would he be so irresponsible?

"I'm not drunk!"

"Then what happened?"

"Drive to your house. I can't talk now. I can't talk now." He leaned forward supporting his head with one hand and the other holding his chest. No one would be able to see him riding in the seat in the dark.

* * *

Lauren relaxed a bit when she was in her garage and the overhead door closed. She was thankful no one had stopped her speeding car. Or maybe she really wanted to get stopped. She would have appreciated the help because she had no idea how she was going to get Chip into her house. He was a lot bigger than she was.

"Okay, Chip. We're here. Can you walk?"

Chip didn't answer. She pushed his shoulder and shook him.

He groaned and opened his eyes. Thank God he was alive.

What was she going to do now?

Lauren grabbed her phone and punched the speed dial number. "Randy, I need you right now. Get over to my house. I'm in the garage. Hurry up." He started to respond, but she clicked off.

The phone rang and it was Randy. Lauren picked up the phone determined not to argue with her brother. "Randy, get over here. I'm in trouble. It's a matter of life and death."

Chapter Fifteen

Randy and Lauren struggled to lug Chip in from the garage. When they dragged him inside, Lauren determined that parking Chip on the lid of the toilet stool was the best place for him. The half bathroom next to the back door was convenient, and the water was right there to clean his wounds.

She almost cried when the bright bathroom light revealed the true extent of Chip's wounds. After tossing the bloody handkerchief into the pink wastebasket, she discovered all the blood had been gushing from a gash right above his left eye. Blood bubbled out of the wound, so she yanked a clean white towel off the rack and pressed it against the wound.

If only she could convince the stubborn man to go to the hospital, but one more suggestion to do so would probably only result in getting him more upset.

"Randy, get him out of his shirt. Let's see how much damage there is to his chest."

Randy unbuttoned the shirt and tried to gently take it off, but Chip groaned in agony. Instead of making him suffer longer, Randy ripped the shirt off as fast as he could.

Chip cried out in pain and nearly fell off the toilet stool. To Lauren's relief, Randy grabbed him and propped him back up. Lauren felt a little guilty now not letting him lie down on her bed or couch.

"Might be some broken ribs in there, buddy. Can you take a deep breath?" Randy said.

Chip tried to sit up straight and took a shallow breath, then a little deeper breath.

"That air bag and seat belt did a number on you, but they probably saved your life. What'd you do, hit a telephone pole?" He threw the soiled shirt into the wastebasket.

Twisting back to Chip, Randy placed his hands on Chip's shoulders to steady him. "What the hell happened anyway?"

"Oh, never mind that right now. Do you think he needs stitches for this?" She pointed to Chip's forehead. The blood still trickled from the gaping gash in his forehead.

Her brother examined Chip's head. "No. We can clean it up. Got any hydrogen peroxide? Probably going to need some gauze and tape to cover it. Hell, I always knew he had a hard head, but this proves it." Randy said.

Chip's face twisted in agony as he knocked Randy's hand away from him. "Quit pressing on it will ya'? Damn, that's sore."

Lauren smiled. Chip was going to be fine.

"I've got some bandages in my medicine cabinet in my bathroom and, oh I wish I had some iodine for that wound." She arched a brow. "That would clean it out good, huh?"

"Quit kiddin' around, will ya'? Get me some aspirins too and a beer. On second thought bring me the beer first."

"The beer will have to wait. I'll grab the other stuff first." she said.

Lauren searched her bathroom medicine chest for the supplies Chip needed. She didn't know if beer and aspirin mixed very well. She'd google it later to be sure.

As she approached the half-bath near the back door, she heard Chip talking to Randy. The irritation in Chip's voice toward her brother stopped her. She paused outside the door to listen.

"No, no, it's nothing like that, Randy. You've got a crazy imagination, that's all," Chip said.

"Maybe you'd better disappear for a while, Chip."

"Hell, I can't hide from them. You know that."

Randy's voice lowered. "You're playing with dangerous people. How can you be so stupid? Tony's dead." Randy said.

"Drop it. Lauren'll hear you. Where is she? My head's killing me and I feel kind of dizzy. I need to lay down."

She waited a minute, trying to calm her fury with those two men. Plastering on a pleasant smile, Lauren pulled out her perfect bedside manner. She was going to find out what happened on that road tonight. Maybe Chip's accident was no *accident* at all.

Chapter Sixteen

The next morning Lauren sat at her kitchen counter sipping hot coffee. Oh how she wanted a cigarette, but she was fighting it. The view through her front window was dazzling with the sun warming up the early morning. The brightness filled her with energy and hope that today would be much better than last night. Her dad had called to tell her that her mother was doing better. So far, no pneumonia.

Now if she could figure out what mischief Chip was in, she'd feel a lot better. Chip slept in the guest room with lots of towels under him to soak up any blood.

She smiled as she turned to check on Randy, his tall frame curled up to fit on the too short couch behind her. What would she have done without him?

He stirred as she watched him. He stretched, almost knocking the lamp off the end table. Opening one eye, then the other, he quickly closed them when the bright sunlight lasered into his eyes.

"Want a cup of coffee to get you going this morning? It's fresh."

Randy sat up on the couch and yawned. "Yeah, after I use the bathroom and check on our patient."

"Okay. He was sleeping when I looked in on him a while ago. Mouth open and snoring, so I know he survived the night." She wasn't really joking. She had been up and down all night to make sure Chip was still alive and breathing. She didn't know if he really was sleeping all night or if he pretended so he didn't have to talk to her.

Lauren sighed. Now that Randy was up, she could stop worrying about watching over Chip. The exhaustion weighed down her body like a heavy blanket. It would have been so much easier on her if she had just taken him to the hospital. Anger flared in the pit of her stomach when she realized Chip manipulated her into doing as he wished...again.

Today was the day of reckoning as far as she was concerned. The discussion she overheard last night between the two men, Chip's refusal to go to the hospital, and his reluctance to explain to her how the accident happened made her suspicious. *What was he trying to get away with now?*

* * *

Lauren heard Randy yell to her from the guest bedroom. "He's awake, Lauren, and ready for some coffee."

Her slippers flip-flopped on the hardwood floor as she carried a steaming mug of coffee to Chip. Her stomach fluttered with nerves, wondering how she was going to coax Chip and Randy into telling her the truth about the wreck last night.

"You look like hell," she said when she handed him the coffee. At least he was sitting up, but his face was swollen. His bare chest and rippling muscles, even if they were bruised, were a pleasant sight to view early this morning.

"Thank you very much. What a great way to be greeted in the morning." He juggled the mug away from Lauren and took a cautious swig of the hot liquid.

"Do you feel like eating anything yet?"

"Maybe in a while. I don't think the accident ruined my appetite." Chip started to pat his stomach, but quickly put his hand back down on the mattress without touching his sore body.

Randy asked, "Did you call for someone to pull out your truck?"

"Yeah, first thing when I woke up this morning. Jorge will bring the trailer out and load it up after he winches it out of the ditch with the tractor. Nobody'll even know it happened."

Lauren leaned closer to Chip. "What are you trying to hide?" Lauren drilled Chip with her eyes, but he wouldn't look up at her. Instead he kept sipping his coffee.

"He's not hiding anything. Slippery roads and he slid off the road. Pretty simple, I'd say." Randy shrugged.

"What's going on, guys? I heard you talking last night. If you weren't high on pot or drunk, which I don't believe you were because you didn't smell like it, what else is it?" She looked from Randy to Chip and back to Randy.

"Are you trying to cover for him, Randy?"

"Don't worry about it, little sister. It's none of your business," Randy said.

"None of my business?" Her eyes flashed with anger. "Who's the one Chip called to come and get him and drag him to my home? Huh? Who's the one who bandaged his wounds and stayed up all night worried to death about him? I certainly *do* have a right to know what's going on."

She pulled back her shoulders and curled her fingers into fists so tight her nails pierced her palms. "I'm worried you guys are in big trouble. And come to think about it, am I in trouble now too?" Again she swept her gaze from one man to the other, daring them not to tell her the truth.

"Is it the money, Chip? You asked me for money and I didn't have it. Who do you owe money to?"

Randy's back stiffened. "You asked my sister for money? Unbelievable." He shook his head. "You are getting desperate."

"All right, yes, I asked her for the money." Facing Lauren, he said, "I've racked up thousands of dollars in debt to the casino. I took a loan out from the farm accounts to pay most of it." He averted his eyes to his mug of coffee.

"What the hell! You're an idiot, Chip." Randy stalked out of the room. The front door slammed behind him.

"So the casino owners are trying to scare you into paying up by running you off the road?"

"Yeah, something like that, I guess." Chip flipped his eyes up to her and took a sip of coffee. His hand touched his bandaged head, and Lauren saw the agony in his face. She wasn't sure if it was caused by the injuries from the crash or from the realization of how much trouble he was in.

"So it's true the Detroit syndicate owns the Castle casino?"

"Yeah, I'm in pretty deep with them, but I know the guys. They won't…"

"You know the guys? Dear God, Chip. How do you know those gangsters?" She moved closer to him. She was afraid to hear the answer to her next question. "Did Tony owe them money too?"

* * *

Gary pulled the cruiser into Lauren's driveway. Not seeing her car in its usual parking place made him wonder if she decided to pull in her garage last night or if something else was up.

120

As he walked up the sidewalk to her front door, his eyes scanned the house and surrounding area. He had to check for sure to see if she was home and okay. It was his job Gary told himself. But he knew in his heart he wanted to have another reason to talk to Lauren and be close to her. His heart beat a little faster as he approached the door. He had to accept the fact that he had regressed to his thirteen-year-old self with raging hormones for a girl he could never have. Chip certainly had all the things a woman would want-money, looks, and power. Three strikes against Gary.

He rapped on the front door and rang the doorbell, giving her a few minutes to answer. He tried again. The thought crossed his mind that perhaps she was just getting out of the shower and would answer the door draped in a towel.

He shook his head. *Officer, control yourself.*

The lock clicked and the door opened only as wide as the security chain allowed, revealing a bit of Lauren's face through the opening, but enough that made his heart leap. She looked pretty cute in the oversized sweatshirt and pajama bottoms printed in colorful smiley faces. Mussed up hair and eyes with smudged mascara added to her early morning look. He could barely contain the grin spreading across his face.

"Gary. What's the matter?" Her eyes reflected fear. Her hand covered her chest.

He cleared his throat and remembered he was a policeman on duty. "Oh, good morning.. I'm just checking because your car wasn't parked out front where you usually park. Everything okay?" He wished she would open the door and let him in. He wanted to hold her and know that she was safe.

"Oh, yeah. It's all good here." Her smile was too big; her eyes did not sparkle.

"Your car okay? In the garage?"

Lauren's gaze darted to the right and up to the ceiling. She took a deep breath and faced Gary through the small opening. "If you recall, Gary, it was raining last night when I got home from the nursing home late. Mom's not well."

"I'm sorry to hear that."

"Well they called this morning and told me she was not any better." She nodded. "So I'm going to get ready and go back there before I go to work."

"Oh, sure. Okay. I'll let you go. I hope she feels better soon." The thirteen-year-old boy was back in his head. He stood there watching her, wishing he could stay with her. Instead, he brushed the brim of his cap and said, "Have a good day."

"Thanks." Lauren shut the door, and the lock latched back in place.

Gary turned away and headed to the cruiser. His head down. What an idiot. Her mother's sick, a killer's loose and he wished her a good day. He'd better get it together and remember he was a police officer not a lovesick teenager.

He strode down the sidewalk to his vehicle and dropped into the driver's seat. Instead of settling in, he watched the house. He wasn't sure what he was looking for, but the vibes he was getting were not good. The look in Lauren's eyes was so unlike her. What was she hiding from him?

Chapter Seventeen

Lauren watched Gary walk back to his cruiser. She hated sneaking around and lying to him.

She pulled on the handle of the front door to be certain it locked and twisted the dead bolt into place. She turned and leaned against the solid door. Gary's visit unnerved her. She felt like the filling in a sandwich crushed between protecting Chip and pretending to Gary that everything was okay.

As Lauren made her way back to the guest bedroom to confront Chip, she stretched her hands over her head a few times and took deep breaths. Head held high, she entered the bedroom and approached Chip sitting up in bed. She targeted his eyes with a piercing gaze, hoping she could see straight into his soul. Was he lying to her?

"Who was at the door," Chip asked when she stopped beside the bed.

"It was Gary wondering where my car was."

"What a pain to be under the microscope of the police, huh?"

"I can see you're not happy they're watching the house."

Chip rolled his eyes. "Makes no difference to me."

"Okay, back to my question. Did Tony owe the syndicate money?"

"Come on, honey." Chip placed his palms up on the bed as if appealing for mercy. "Drop it. I don't know if Tony owed the guys money or not." He picked at a thread on the dark blue sheet that covered him.

"Don't honey me, Chip. You're lying." Lauren's eyes narrowed. She braced herself to not give in to Chip's smooth talk. "You and Tony were friends, or I thought you were. You know if he was in trouble with the syndicate."

Chip winced as he sat up straighter against the pillows. "Forget it, Lauren. Quit buggin' me." He dropped his forehead into his hands and groaned. "The subject is closed." He threw off the sheet and struggled to sit upright on the side of the bed.

"I'm not dropping it. Tony was our friend. I want to know who killed him." She waited for Chip to start talking, but he only rested on the bed holding his damaged body up with a hand flat against the mattress on each side of him. She was torn between wanting to shake the truth out of him till his teeth rattled and rushing to hug him to soothe the pain in his injured body.

"And you think I know? You're crazy." He stood up with his back to Lauren, but quickly put his hand back on the head board to steady his upright body.

Lauren stepped away from him, now half-hoping he'd fall because he was so not cooperating with her.

She folded her arms against her chest. "You're the one who's crazy here. You can't be messing around with these dangerous gangsters. You need to go to the police and tell them what happened. I'll drive you to the police station or call Gary for you. Whatever you want." Clasping her hands together, she waited, and hoped he would decide to go to the police. She didn't want to report the accident.

Chip turned around. His face was white and twisted in pain. "You really are out of your ever-lovin' mind to think I'm going to the police. You don't understand, Lauren. You don't know half of it."

"Then tell me, Chip." She moved to him and grabbed his arm to support him as he tried to walk a few steps. She shook her head as she looked at his injured body and thought he was about as strong as a kitten.

"No. You're not getting involved." He stopped. His eyes focused on her. "The only place you're driving me is to my house."

"Don't you get it? I am involved! The minute you called me to pick you up." She let go of his arm. Let him fall. "So you owe me an explanation. What if whoever ran you off the road is watching us? Watching me?" She pointed to her chest. "So now what? What are you going to do?"

Chip blinked. "Don't be such a drama queen. I have a plan. Take me home." She searched his bruised and bandaged face. He was just as stubborn as she was.

"Fine! Let's go," she said. "But this is not the end of the discussion."

"As far as I'm concerned, it is," he said in an emphatic voice.

"Come on. You're going home." She matched his angry voice and strode from the room without looking back.

* * *

After leaving Lauren's house, Gary was restless and angry. He had to find out what the Detective knew about Tony's murder so he could prove Lauren and her family were innocent. He practically crushed the steering wheel on the way to police headquarters as he remembered how Richards kept accusing Lauren, her brother, and father of murder.

Enraged by the detective's statements Gary stormed into Detective Richards' office and let go of all the fury that had built up inside of him during the drive.

"Lauren doesn't know a thing about the pot deliveries." Gary planted his feet on the floor determined to make a case for Lauren's innocence.

Detective Richards threw his pen down on his desk and stood up. "You have no evidence to back that up, do you, Officer? Don't get pissed at me for suspecting Lauren is tied up in the drug deals."

He placed his hands on the desktop and leaned toward Gary. "Tony's the one who told us the funeral home is the pick-up point for the dealers. Lauren works at the funeral home. It's that simple. How can she not know about it?" He straightened up, a vein in his neck pulsing.

Gary's eyes widened in surprise. He had never heard about Tony being a snitch.

"When did Tony give up that information?"

"It's been a couple of months since we picked him up for selling pot. He didn't want to go to jail, so we made a deal with him if he turned in evidence against the dealers and top level guys."

"Why didn't you go in and bust all of them right away? It could've saved his life."

"I understand that, but Tony was wired to collect evidence for us so we could get the head man in the operation. But they must've gotten on to him. We don't have anyone else on the inside to spring the trap on the top man. He's a smart guy."

"And who is it?" Gary leaned in to hear the answer.

"You know I can't tell you that." Richards glanced away.

"So you're telling me because Tony said the funeral home is a pick up point? That's why you think Lauren, her dad, and Randy are in on it?" Gary shook his head in disbelief. He couldn't imagine Mr. Staab as a drug dealer. "Hell, you might as well conclude that her mother with Alzheimer's is also in on it!"

The detective moved around his desk and stood toe-to-toe with Gary. "What is it? Are you getting sweet on the girl? Now that will really cloud your brain."

Shaking his head, Gary said, "Come on. Lauren can't be in on it. That's crazy and you know it." He punctuated each word with his fist.

"You're too close to this family to be objective. You're officially off the case. We'll assign someone else to watch Miss Staab. "Richards turned his back on Gary and moved toward his desk.

"Unbelievable." Gary threw up his hands. "You need me. You don't have enough cops in this town to cover security at the high school basketball games, let alone to protect this family from a murderer and drug dealers. You can't take me off this case."

The detective swung around to face Gary. "That's enough, Officer Applegate." The detective's eyes narrowed. "An outburst like that could go into your personnel files. Discussion closed. The chief will re-assign you effective now."

Chapter Eighteen

After dropping off Chip at the farm, Lauren raced toward the nursing home. On her way, she argued with herself about being angry at Chip. Even if he wouldn't tell her the whole story behind the car crash, she still cared about the big lug.

They had some great times together and not just in bed. He could be a lot of fun, thoughtful, and caring. But was it only when he needed something from her? She rolled her eyes. Or was she the one taking advantage of Chip? He wined and dined her, and yet she couldn't imagine settling down with him, raising a family, and growing old together. She frowned at the thought. Why was she thinking about getting old?

Enough about Chip, she had to focus on her mother. She wheeled into the parking lot of the nursing facility. Gripping the steering wheel tightly, she let the motor run. When she turned it off, she'd have to face the reality of seeing her mother ill and weak. That's what made her think about growing old.

She grabbed her bag and finally let the idea surface from her brain and show its ugly side. As she locked the car and turned toward the facility, she faced the possibility of a future of living with Alzheimer's like her mother had endured. Pulling herself together, she forged ahead to another visit with her mom.

"Good morning, Lauren." June greeted her as she walked down the hall, but not with her usual big smile.

"What's wrong, June?" Lauren didn't want to take time for pleasantries. She could see the tension in June's demeanor.

"Glad you're here. She slept off and on last night, but seems to be stronger this morning. No fever now." June smiled and held Lauren's hands, squeezing them gently. They continued walking together down the hall to her mother's room. June opened the door allowing Lauren to enter first. She stood there a moment with Lauren. "If you need me for anything, please call me. Okay?" June touched her shoulder, and left when Lauren nodded.

Sitting down at her mother's bed side, Lauren shivered in the unusually cool room. She sneezed three quick sneezes.

"Henry, you're here aren't you." His shadow drifted into view.

"Yes, I am." His voice was quieter than she had ever heard it. "I've been here all night with her."

Her mother coughed, not once but three times. Coughs that sounded like they came all the way up from her toes. "Mom, it's Lauren. I'm here." She grasped her mother's hand and hung on.

"Lauren, oh dear Lauren." Her mother's raspy voice was barely audible. She kept her eyes closed. "Henry still here?"

"Yes, dear, all night." Henry said.

Opening her eyes, her mother moved her head on the pillow, lips curving upward into a smile.

Lauren's eyebrows shot up in surprise as she turned her gaze on Henry. "She knows you're here." Her voice was a whisper. "My mother can see you too?" Henry moved his hands behind his back and stood straighter.

"So if we both know you're actually standing here, I'm not dreaming this." Her hand covered her heart. Her mind swirled trying to absorb this mind-boggling reality.

He nodded his head. "I'm not a dream, Lauren. I'm really in the room with both of you." His silhouette hovered near her. "There was a time when I actually walked on the earth as a real man."

Lauren blinked. "But now you're a shadow? What happened?" She stood up. "Why are you here with my mom?"

"Hold on, Lauren. One question at a time, please." He stopped. "Your father's coming down the hall." His shadow began to fade. "Please know, I am here to help, not for evil. You need not worry about your mother."

Chapter Nineteen

After leaving her mother's room, Lauren's head was filled with the image of her mom lying in the hospital bed. She seemed so small in that huge bed.

She shook her head. Was Henry really there and they both talked with him? She swallowed hard. Wait, maybe she dozed off a bit and dreamed all three of them were conversing in her mother's room. It wasn't real. It couldn't have been real.

She gripped her car's steering wheel tighter to help her forget that preposterous visit and to focus on the work day ahead of her. The responsibilities for providing the funeral service for a family that afternoon were on her shoulders because her dad wanted to stay with her mother.

Lauren was relieved to see Norma's car parked in the lot at the funeral home. Thank goodness Norma and her husband would be around to help. They were dependable and good family friends. A light bulb flashed in Lauren's mind. Yes, Norma knew her mother very well. A sly smile etched her face.

She opened the front door of the funeral home and did a double take. Norma's husband,

Delbert, was holding the step ladder while Norma was on the top rung stretching ever so precariously to screw a light bulb into the foyer chandelier.

"Norma, don't you be breaking your neck now by falling off that ladder." Lauren rushed to help the short, bald-headed Delbert hang on to the aluminum ladder. "Be careful," she said as she got an up close vantage point of Norma's skinny white legs on full display under her red shorts.

"Got it." She sighed with relief as she dropped her arms from the secured light bulb and shook them to get the blood flowing back to her hands.

Peering down at Lauren, she said, "I was dusting the chandelier and this bulb decided to flicker out." Nodding her head at Delbert, she said, "Turn on the light, hon, and see if it works now." Wearing his usual pair of denim overalls, he stepped to the wall by the entry door and flipped on the switch.

"Aha, let there be light," he said. Sure enough. The chandelier glowed brightly and the recently cleaned crystal shades sparkled.

"Beautiful." Lauren choked back a clot in her throat when she remembered how proud her mother was when she found the antique light fixture. Wired for electricity, visitors usually commented on the beauty of it and how appropriate it was for the Victorian styled house.

Lauren and Delbert held the ladder as Norma clambered down. As soon as her feet touched the floor, she twisted to face Lauren. "How's your mom? Any improvement?"

"Yes, the fever's gone. That's a good thing." Lauren tried to make her voice sound hopeful.

Norma's eyes misted over. She gave Lauren a huge hug, like she used to do when Lauren was a kid.

"Now, can I finish setting up the chairs in the front room," Delbert asked after the pair's embrace. He patted Lauren's shoulder when Norma nodded her head. "Thank you, my darling." He winked at Lauren as he sauntered into the other room.

"I wish you could visit Mom, but the doctor doesn't want anybody in except family right now." She watched as Norma pulled a tissue from her pocket and slipped it behind her glasses to dry her eyes. "I know how close you guys are to each other. You're family to us."

"Thank you, sweetie." She patted Lauren's arm.

"Mom was re-visiting the past a bit this morning."

Hoping her mother would forgive her for the little lie, she decided to push on to ask the one person who knew her mother for years. "She was talking about a man named Henry." She chewed her lip. "Do you remember anybody named Henry?"

Norma's brows shot up into her forehead. "Oh, yes, I do." She turned toward the ladder. "Now wouldn't you think Delbert would be back to pick this ladder up and put it away for us?" She began to fold up the ladder.

"Leave it. Randy'll be through here in a minute. We don't need to drag it to the garage. We have plenty of other things to get done before the service later this afternoon."

"I guess you're right there."

"So who is Henry? I've never heard Mom talk about him before. Do I know him?" She hoped she sounded convincing.

"Oh, I doubt it." Norma glanced up toward the organ in the corner of the room. She seemed to be very interested in checking to see if the organ was dusty.

"Is he from around here?" Lauren put her hands behind her back and rocked forward and back telling herself not to push too hard for answers. She didn't want Norma suspicious about her bringing up Henry at this time.

"No, no. Not at all. He was a friend, her good friend." Norma grabbed the chandelier's dead light bulb from the chair where Delbert had left it. "Delbert goes off and leaves everything. He'd forget his socks and underwear if I didn't remind him." She grinned at Lauren, then her face turned sober.

"It was pretty tough on Barbara when Henry died."

"Oh my goodness. Was he ill?"

"No, unfortunately, he was in a car wreck. His car went off the road near the bridge over Jenkins Creek."

The air in Lauren's lungs whooshed out of her. "Did you say he crashed near Jenkins Creek?" That was the same location where Chip was run off the road.

"Yes, it'd been raining quite hard. I think the investigators decided he must have been going too fast and slid off into the ditch. No one else was involved in the accident, thank goodness."

Lauren's face paled. She stood motionless as if she had been glued to the floor.

"Are you okay, hon?" Norma moved next to her. "You look like you've seen a ghost."

Chapter Twenty

Lauren blinked back her thoughts of the coincidence between the location of both Chip and Henry's car crashes. "I'm okay." She flipped her bangs to the side of her head.

Randy loped into the entryway carrying four folding chairs, two at each side. Resting them on the floor, he looked to Lauren like the little brother she remembered coming home troubled about a lost kitten. His usual bright eyes seemed dark and full of sadness. "Hey, Sis, how's Mom doing?"

"She's better. No fever."

Randy nodded. "I'm going over there as soon as I get the room set up for the service." He picked up the chairs. "The florist just dropped off a few more plants and flowers." He jerked his head toward the garage. "Can you set them up?"

"No problem," Lauren said.

"I can help her with those flowers." Norma patted her on her back. "I'm glad to see the color come back in your face."

"Thanks. Do you want to grab the flowers and bring them in? I'll have to get more stands from the garage storage." Norma nodded, and the women headed toward the garage.

It was good to do something to take her mind off her mother and the puzzle about Henry. She might even be able to pump Norma for more information about him while setting up the flowers.

When they opened the door connecting the house to the garage, she spotted two colorful arrangements of flowers and a dish garden of green plants in the flower delivery area. Norma checked the cards to see if they were family pieces while Lauren moved on to the back of the garage where the flower stands were stored.

"These arrangements are too big to handle more than one at a time. I'll be back to get the other flowers and dish garden," Norma said.

"Good idea."

Lauren pulled open the padlock that supposedly kept the closet secure. It was only dummy locked so anyone could easily get into it, but a stranger would never know the padlock was not actually clicked into the lock. She slid the door of the closet open to reach the stands. To make a pleasing display to showcase the flowers' beauty, she needed stands of varying heights. She tugged on a few of them, but they were wedged into the closet so tightly, she couldn't move them. Now that was crazy. They were never so piled and pushed together like this.

She slid the doors to the other side of the track and discovered boxes of embalming fluid stored on that side of the closet. She huffed in disgust at Randy's laziness. Instead of carrying the cardboard containers upstairs for storage in the prep room closet, he packed them away in here. She shook her head. There must have been a fantastic sale on embalming fluid to order this many cases.

The only thing to do was to move some of them out into the garage so she could make room to pull out the flower stands. Randy was definitely going to hear about this!

Lauren put both arms around a box and wiggled it off the top of the stack. When she lifted it, she nearly threw it up to the ceiling. It was so light compared to the usual weight of a case of embalming fluid. The bottles inside weren't even shifting as usual. Certainly a major Improvement in packaging. Upon closer examination, she noticed the box was pretty beat up and had been opened and re-taped with silver duct tape. Staring at the packaging, her curiosity piqued.

She moved to the tool bench and picked up a box opener and returned, slicing through the duct tape. When she pulled back the cardboard top, an earthy smell assaulted her senses. She slapped her hand to her mouth. Oh no. Oh no.

"Damn it, Lauren! What are you doing?" She jerked her head around to see Randy standing in the doorway. His angry face frightened her.

"What am I doing?" She straightened her back and waved her hand at the boxes in the closet and the one on the floor. "What are *you* doing?"

"You shouldn't be messin' around in that closet. Those cases are none of your business." He marched toward her.

Norma appeared at the door eying the two of them. "Everything okay, kids?"

Lauren's eyes flashed up to Norma as she tried to control her trembling voice. "Everything's fine. Randy needs to help me with these boxes and flower stands." Randy picked up the box and replaced it in the closet.

"I'll be in with the stands in a minute. Thanks so much for hauling all those pieces in." Turning away from Norma, Lauren shoved the sliding door away from the stands so Randy could reach and pull them out.

"What the hell are you thinking," she asked in a hushed voice. "Hiding boxes of pot in here?"

Randy didn't answer or even acknowledge her. He jerked a stack of stands out of the closet.

"Randy." Rage seethed through her body. "What are these boxes of pot doing here?" she asked through clenched teeth.

"Forget it." He slammed the stands down on the concrete floor and stalked out of the garage.

Forget it. Forget it? She placed her hands on the side of her head and squeezed tightly. What in the world was Randy doing?

Grabbing the flower stands, Lauren practically flew through the funeral home, dropping them off in the chapel area, and rushed into the casket room. She pulled the door closed behind her and speed-walked to the casket she remembered she had latched when cleaning earlier. Her heart racing, she raised the lids at the head and the foot of the casket. Sniffing deeply, Lauren recognized the faint smell, but where was it coming from? She threw the casket stole on the floor and pitched the pillow on top of it. Beginning at the foot of the casket, she pulled away the flimsy mattress. Small bags of marijuana were encased in larger plastic bags and packed into the underside of the casket floor.

The scream of outrage almost escaped her lips, stifled only by pressing both hands over her mouth. Lauren's eyes widened in horror. Randy was bold enough to hide the marijuana inside a casket? She whirled away from the gray-upholstered coffin and glanced around the room. Were all of them packed full of weed?

Now was not the time to tear each casket apart to look. She had to get ready to conduct a funeral for the grieving family who would be arriving at any minute.

Lauren covered the bags of marijuana with the mattress and picked up the materials and tossed them back into the casket. After closing the lids, she swung her arms around the area to help dispel the odor of the marijuana.

Perhaps the perfume from the funeral flowers would cover up that odor. She could only hope.

Chapter Twenty-One

Gary drove by the funeral home late in the afternoon and noted everyone had left after the funeral service. When he saw only Lauren's car parked in the lot, his face flooded red with anger. He had warned her not to be alone. The city police patrolled the area, but he knew their police force wasn't large enough to afford her the protection she needed. Even with the County Sheriff Deputies patrolling the streets of Mayfield after midnight when the city police shift ended, there was no way they could cover the entire county and spend that much time watching her and her family's activities.

Gary pulled into the parking lot. He would have to warn her again. His scowl turned into a smile. The thought of being with her energized his body. He wanted to see her, breathe in her scent, touch her.

He emerged from the cruiser and pulled his cap down tightly on his head. He didn't care if the chief took him off the case. He had to check on her. He slammed and locked the door and reached the front door of the funeral home in record time.

Gary started to knock, then tried the antique door handle. It clicked and he pushed the door open. He bristled at the idea the door was not even locked. When he entered through the doorway, a gentle bell rang to announce visitors.

"Lauren," he called. He walked into the dimly lighted foyer and squinted as he searched the area for her. "Lauren," he repeated but louder this time. His heart began to beat in his throat. "Are you here? Anybody here?"

"Gary?" She closed the door to the casket room quickly and walked to him in her bare feet. Her cheeks flushed a shade of red.

"Lauren. Are you alright?" Forgetting he was a cop on duty, he cupped her chin and tilted her face up toward him.

She sniffed a bit and fell against his chest. His arms wrapped around her and held her tightly as she cried against him. Concern replaced his anger with her for being alone.

He couldn't stop himself from cradling her in his arms and pressing his lips into her hair. As he gently rocked her back and forth, her floral fragrance sent ribbons of chills spiraling over his skin. She clung tightly to him as if clinging to a lifesaver.

He asked in a whisper above her bowed head, "What's happened?"

Lauren stepped away from him. She hesitated for a minute. "It's my mom."

Oh dear God in Heaven. He reached for her hands and held on tightly.

"She's been sick. But she doesn't have a fever anymore. She's much better."

"Well, that's good news, isn't it?" He was perplexed. She was crying because of good news? He shook his head. Women's emotions always baffled him.

"Yes, very good news. When I left her this morning, I was so worried she would get pneumonia." She stopped, inhaled, and released a ragged breath. "What a relief to know she's improving." Lauren's watery eyes gazed into his. "It's been a very difficult day. Hold me again."

She snuggled against his chest and her warmth filled him with joy. The only sounds in the room were the ticking of the antique grandfather's clock and her breathing. He could have stayed there forever with Lauren in his arms.

She turned her face up to him and he lightly brushed her lips with his. She moved her hands behind his neck and pulled him to her lips once again. He kissed her deeply. His senses were on fire, and the center of his heart soared when she matched his passion.

Gary lifted his face away from her and studied her glistening eyes. Her lips turned up when she gazed into his face.

"Hey what's that smile on your face," he asked. He couldn't help but reflect the smile with his own.

"Well, my mother's better, but that's not the reason why I'm happy now." She held him and they swayed back and forth again. "I think

you're a policeman and you can figure it out."
Her grin lit up the whole room.

"Um, let me see. Let's try that again to make sure I'm following the right leads on this case." He bent down again and devoured her mouth pulling her tightly against his pulsating body.

After that long embrace, Lauren reached for Gary's hand and led him into the family room.

"I'm going over to see Mom. I was cleaning up after the service here this afternoon. But I could use a cup of coffee to pick me up, although I'd say the kisses and snuggling actually revitalized me." An impish grin flicked across her face.

"Technically I'm on duty right now, but coffee would be okay." His eyebrow arched as a rakish smile spread into his eyes. She pulled him into the family room motioning him to sit on the couch.

"Um, Lauren, I have a confession to make." He placed his hands on her shoulders and engaged her eyes with his. "I don't drink coffee."

"You what? After the times I've fixed you coffee or offered you coffee?" Her face broke into a huge grin. She tapped his chin with her finger. "Then why did you say coffee would be okay and follow me in here, Officer?"

"Would you believe me if I told you I was just following leads in the case?"

"Oh, right." She giggled and he felt his blood burn through his body.

* * *

Even with the warmth of Gary's body hugging her, Lauren felt the cool air surge in around her and her nose tickle. Sure signs that Henry was in the room. She stood on tiptoe to look over Gary's shoulder and glance around the room.

The coffee maker began gurgling. She stepped back from Gary when she heard it, then realized she hadn't even turned on the machine. Rushing around the couch, she flicked the switch off. Clenching her fists at her sides, she looked again for the shadow man. This wasn't the time for one of Henry's pranks.

Turning and smiling at Gary, she said, "Huh, that crazy coffee pot must have a short in it. Starting up like that." She unplugged it from the wall. "I'll have to pick up another one." As she walked away from the counter, the basket of coffee creamer packages fell to the floor.

Lauren's eyes closed as she concentrated on keeping her composure in front of Gary. Did she hear Henry snickering in the background?

She quickly walked to the other end of the counter and stooped to pick up the packets. Gary joined her picking up the basket, turning it over, and scooping up more packets. Their hands went for the same packet, but instead of grabbing the creamer package, Gary covered Lauren's hand with his and crouched down across from her. His hot gaze mesmerized her. Still holding her hand, he pulled her up and kicked away the basket between them. Her body's heat index soared when his mouth engulfed her lips as they held each other.

The unplugged coffee maker began gurgling again. They didn't notice.

Chapter Twenty-Two

Gary walked Lauren to her car parked outside the funeral home. "Thanks for the coffee." He winked and opened the car door for her.

"Sure. I know how much you love coffee." Her eyes sparkled when she grinned back at him. Sitting down in the driver's seat and throwing her purse in the passenger seat, she could feel him consuming her with his eyes as she slid her long bare legs in under the steering wheel. She reached for the seat belt and pulled it around her.

He leaned in and said, "I'll follow you to the nursing home. "

"Okay, thanks." She pulled the bunch of keys from her purse and pushed one into the ignition. He slammed the door and moved to his cruiser which was parked beside her car.

The cell phone jangled alive breaking her pleasant aura. Emmett. Lauren rolled her eyes, wanting to ignore his call. Emmett got on her nerves, but she steeled herself to be nice to him to get the information about the marijuana deals.

She pressed the answer button. "Hi, Emmett."

"Hey, Lauren. How ya' doin'." The sound of his voice made her skin crawl. To think he could possibly be selling dope to kids was too difficult to even imagine.

"I'm okay. What's up?"

"Checking in to see if you've talked to Chip lately. I need to talk to him."

"No, I haven't seen him for a while. Sorry I can't help you. Did you call Randy?" She pinched her lips together. She hoped Randy didn't tell him anything about Chip's truck crash by Jenkins Creek.

"Yeah, he hasn't seen him either. Okay." He hesitated. "Where are you?"

"I'm heading over to see my mom at the nursing home. She's pretty sick. Was Randy there when you talked to him?"

"Oh, I don't know. Didn't ask."

The phone clicked off. Lauren was sick of Emmett's ill manners and intrusion in her life.

She looked out her window at Gary who waited patiently in the cruiser. She mouthed "sorry" to him and held up her phone.

As she drove to the nursing home Lauren anticipated meeting her dad and Randy there so they could fill her in on her mother's condition. Maybe she'd be awake enough to visit with her. The gloom descended on her like a heavy blanket. Why did she have to build up her hopes only to come back to the reality that her mother was improving physically, but she would never recover from Alzheimer's?

* * *

When Lauren entered her mother's room, the stillness was what hit her first. In the dim light, she saw her dad in the chair and her mother in the bed. No sounds at all. That was a good thing, she thought. She was breathing quietly. Lauren smiled. What relief.

She closed the door softly behind her. Her dad's head was down and he was napping in the straight chair. She could only imagine how exhausted he was after sitting by her mother's bedside for hours. Dealing with her dementia and illness had to be stressful for him.

She tip-toed to the side of the bed. Her mother's color was good. She was resting peacefully. Lauren wanted to hug and kiss her. Instead of disturbing her sleep, she sat down in the recliner chair nearby. It felt good to have some peace and quiet.

As she settled into the seat of the chair, Lauren realized she was smiling. Smiling knowing her mother was recovering, but also because thoughts of Gary's kisses and passion filled the center of her heart. She sat straight up in the chair. Was she feeling love for Gary?

Her father wiggled in his chair and his head came up, then dropped again to his chest. He looked so uncomfortable.

"Dad," she whispered. She scooted out of the recliner and tapped him on his shoulder. "Daddy."

He breathed in a deep breath and snorted. She stifled a giggle at the noise. He opened his eyes wide. She knew by his expression he couldn't figure out where he was in his half-awake state.

"Shhh." She placed her finger in front of her lips. "Mom's asleep. Why don't you go home and get some rest?"

He ran the palm of his hand from his forehead all the way down to his chin. "Oh, yeah." His eyes brightened when he saw Lauren. "How long you been here?"

"Only a few minutes. I'll stay with Mom. Go home and get some rest, will you?"

He glanced over to his wife who was still sleeping and gazed back at Lauren. "It's been tough." His voice cracked with emotion. "But she's going to be fine." Tears pooled in his eyes.

"I don't know what I'll ever do without her," he said. He dropped his gaze to the floor.

Lauren bent over and hugged her father around his shoulders. She didn't want to let go of him, hoping her embrace would give him strength. He flicked the tears from his eyes.

"She's good now, Dad. She's breathing easily." Lauren stood up. "You go home and rest. Norma brought some lasagna over for you and Randy. It's in the refrigerator, well, unless Randy beat you home and ate all of it first."

"Oh yes, that would be Randy." He glanced at his watch. "He's been gone about an hour. I hope there's a bite left."

"Well he wasn't at the funeral home when I left. Probably stopped for a burger."

He stood up and walked over to her mother. Placing a kiss on his fingertips, he lightly touched his wife's forehead. "Good night, Barb."

Turning to Lauren, he said, "Tell her I'll be back early in the morning, okay?"

"Sure, Dad. Will do." He opened the door and quietly closed it behind him. They both knew Barbara wouldn't remember him being there or Lauren telling her he would return in the morning.

Lauren sat back in the recliner, rested her head on the head rest, and closed her eyes. She felt so drowsy. In her half-awake condition, she felt the back of the recliner for an afghan. The air conditioning must have kicked on because there was a definite chill in the air. Three quick sneezes brought her wide awake.

Her eyes darted to her mother lying in the bed. Thank goodness her silly sneezes didn't disturb her.

"Lauren. Are you awake enough to talk to me?"

Without moving from the chair, she responded, "Yes, Henry. Now I am." She massaged the sides of her head with her fingers.

Her eyes popped open when she realized she wasn't talking out loud to Henry. How did they communicate? Oh, right, he's a shadow. What an absurd situation—telecommunicating with a shadow. She pinched her arm and it hurt. Unfortunately she wasn't dreaming.

Chapter Twenty-Three

Lauren glanced again at her mother to see if she was awakened by Henry's presence. She twisted her body to face Henry's dark silhouette hovering by the recliner.

"I talked to Norma about you this afternoon. She told me you were a very good friend of my mother's." Lauren hesitated. Perhaps she shouldn't dig up the past, so to speak, to learn of his history when he was a live, real person and interacting with her mother.

"Yes, we were very good friends," Henry answered with a tinge of sadness in his voice. Lauren felt the air in the room warm when he mentioned her mother. "Norma was right."

"I don't remember you." Lauren frowned.

"You were just a baby."

"How did you two meet?"

"At a visitation at the funeral home for my great aunt many years ago." His voice sounded lighter as he recalled their first meeting. "My aunt took care of me from the time I was ten years old. When my father left my mother, she decided she didn't really want to care for me anymore. Aunt Doris volunteered to take me in.

Besides knowing your mom, Aunt Doris was the best thing that ever happened to me."

"My mother was as important to you as the woman who raised you?" Lauren's brow wrinkled. "That's an odd thing to say."

"Because I loved your mother, Lauren."

"Everybody loves my mom." She smiled remembering how easily her mother made friends. She was always doing something for someone.

"And she truly loved me," Henry replied. "We were good for each other."

Lauren nodded her head thinking she and Gary were good for each other too. "It's great to have close friends," she said.

Henry moved in front of Lauren, his shadow growing darker it seemed. "We were more than good friends. She made me happy and I tried to do all I could to make her happy too."

Lauren's eyes narrowed and she leaned toward the shadow. "What are you telling me?"

Henry floated to one side of the room, then returned and stopped so close to Lauren, she could feel his tension in her own body.

"I have to tell you, Lauren, I asked her to leave your father and marry me."

Lauren bolted upright in the recliner. "You're not serious. You're trying to pull another prank, aren't you, Henry?" Please, please, please, let it be a joke.

"No, my dear. It isn't a joke. We discussed Barbara leaving your father so we could get married."

Lauren shook her head and covered her ears. "I don't want to hear anymore." She bit her lip realizing she would hear him anyway through their thoughts.

She wished she hadn't even asked him how he met her mother or quizzed Norma to discover her mother and Henry were good friends. "Good friends." She snorted. Did Norma know about their relationship?

If Henry were telling her the truth, her childhood was a lie. The perfect family she thought she had was a sham.

She could still sense his presence next to her. She wanted to throw him out of the room, but how do you toss out a shadow?

"I know it's a difficult idea to comprehend. We loved each other before you were born. I never wanted to leave her, but the car wreck ended my future on Earth and any chance to stay with her."

Lauren rocketed out of the chair. "Get out of here! You're disturbing me and my mother." Lauren heard the sharp tone in her voice. She glanced over at her mother who was stirring from her sleep.

"Now look what you've done, Henry. Mom's waking up." Lauren stood up and rushed to her mother's bedside. "It's okay, Mom. Go back to sleep." She touched her shoulder and slid her hand down her arm to her mother's hand.

Barbara peered back at her. "Henry? Is Henry here?"

"Yes, darling, I'm right here."

Lauren's jaw dropped. How dare he call her darling. "Mom, do you want Henry to stay?"

"Yes, of course, he must stay with me. We should be together. He loves me and I love him." Her mother's eyes looked clear and sparkling.

Lauren dropped her mother's hand and twirled to look at the shadow. "What have you done to my mother? What are you, a demon who has invaded my mother's mind?" She placed her hand on her churning stomach.

"Lauren, I told you I'm here for good, not evil. I've been waiting for your mother for years because we love each other." When Henry glided to the side of the bed, Lauren backed away from him.

"All those years ago, I asked her to come with me, but she refused. She couldn't leave you kids to grow up without her. She loved you all too much to run away."

"Impossible, Henry. I don't believe one word of what you said!" She raised her voice. "Stop it. Stop it now." She clenched her fists to her side and felt the fury twist her insides. "My mother would never betray my father."

"Lauren. Leave him alone." The stern voice of her childhood brought Lauren to attention. Her mother's effort brought on a

157

round of coughing and choking. Lauren pressed the call button and ran to the door and opened it. She shouted down the hallway, "My mother. Hurry. Mother needs help. Someone help us."

A nurse and an aide ran into the room. Lauren stayed back and let the team do what they had to do to calm her and ease the coughing.

She scanned the room for a sign of Henry because she could feel his presence. She breathed deeply with a sense of relief that at least he was staying in the background.

Lauren refused to believe him. Her mom would never consider leaving her dad for him. She dropped her gaze to the floor as her shoulders slumped. The tears filled her eyes and spilled down her cheeks. If only she hadn't asked how he knew her mother.

* * *

Lauren sat by her mother's bedside with an unopened magazine on her lap. She couldn't concentrate on reading when all she could think about was the possibility of her mother's affair with Henry.

"Lauren." Her mother's soft voice broke into her thoughts.

"Yes, Mom, I'm here." She stood up and reached for her hand.

"Are you alone?" Her mother tightly clasped her hand in hers and squeezed it gently.

"Yes." Lauren dreaded what her mother would have to say now.

"You know how much I love you, don't you? I love you and your brother with all my heart."

"Sure I do." She perched herself on the side of the bed to get closer. She was amazed at how lucid she seemed after so many years of her mind being broken and lost in the midst of the Alzheimer's disease.

"I need to explain some things to you before I go."

"Before you go? Where are you going?" Lauren shook her head. Not as lucid as she thought.

"Your dad and I, like all marriages, had a few bumps to stumble over. And we had some major arguments and disagreements that drove us apart." She squeezed Lauren's hand again. "I always loved him, but there were times when I didn't like him much." She smiled at Lauren.

Lauren crinkled her brow. "I remember hearing some of those disagreements." She wiggled her fingers in the air to frame the word with quotation marks. "Randy and I usually hunkered under the dining room table to stay out of the way."

"Your father never hit me or hurt me during those arguments." Her mother fixed her gaze on Lauren.

"No, but it did get pretty loud sometimes, and then he would stomp out of the room." She squeezed her eyes tight trying to erase the memory of those frightening moments.

"We fought through most of those years of our early marriage, even before you and your brother came along. It was during one of those periods of anger and hurt that I met Henry." Lauren caught her breath, wanting, but not wanting, to know about Henry and their relationship.

"He was very kind. He paid attention to me and gave me lovely, expensive gifts." She cleared her throat. "Look in my jewelry box on the dresser and bring the open heart necklace over here," her mother instructed.

Lauren knew exactly which necklace her mother described. Opening the lid of the box, she picked up the delicate heart on the fine gold chain. The sparkle from the sprinkle of diamonds on the edge of the heart caught her eye. She remembered seeing the necklace in her mother's jewelry box and loving it since she was a girl, but she frowned when she realized she had never seen her mother actually wearing it.

Walking back to her mother's bedside, she said, "I have the necklace. It's so beautiful. Do you want me to put it on you?"

"No, honey. Henry gave it to me and now, I want you to have it."

"Why? Why would I want something from him?" Lauren clenched the delicate jewelry in the palm of her hand. "He means nothing to me and he certainly doesn't mean anything to you anymore." She felt the anger crawling up her throat. "Does he?"

Her mother scooted back in the bed and sat up. Her gaze dropped to her hands resting in her lap.

Struggling to control her disappointment and surprise, Lauren asked, "Why would you even keep this?" She gazed once again at the delicate golden heart in her hand. The disbelief grew along with her fury. Surely her mother was not thinking clearly. She has to be confused to even think Henry was her lover. Her mother could never betray her father. It was the Alzheimer's. It had twisted her mind.

"I want you to keep it because it was given to me by your father," she said.

"Mother, you aren't making sense at all. You just said Henry gave you the necklace, not Daddy." She smiled with relief realizing her mother was confused after all.

"No, Lauren."

She covered Lauren's clenched fist with her hand. "Henry is your real father."

Lauren's eyes widened. Taking a breath, she said, "You really need some rest, Mom. You're not making sense at all."

"It's true, Lauren."

Recognizing Henry's voice, she whirled around to face him. She gasped and covered her mouth with her hands when she saw his shadow fading and a handsome man emerging from the filmy shape. A dapper gray suit fit his slender body and Henry's familiar fedora was on his head and his raincoat slung over one arm He placed the umbrella at his side. His gorgeous blue eyes softened as he watched her.

Lauren trembled. She was going to pass out, when she realized she was looking into blue eyes like her own.

She backed away a few steps and blinked. In that fraction of an instant, she saw her mother standing at his side. Lauren shook her head to clear her vision. She caught her breath. Her mother was no longer that sick old woman in the bed, but rather the young and attractive woman Lauren remembered when she was a child. Dressed in her favorite yellow sundress and sandals, her mother put her arm through Henry's. The joy on her face brightened the room.

"Mom?" She stood completely still afraid her vision was playing tricks on her and willed her knees not to buckle on her now.

"Yes, honey. It's me." She pointed to her chest and bent down in a flamboyant bow. Her eyes radiated her happiness as she stood up straight again.

Lauren nodded her head as she tried to comprehend what was happening.

"It's time to say good-bye to this life and start a new one in another time together with Henry. We were always meant to be together, and now we can."

"But what about Dad? He loves you, and I thought you loved him?" Lauren choked on the words and could not continue.

"I do love your father, Lauren. I always have. I know it sounds impossible to you to love two men, but my heart is deep and full of love to share with each man." She turned to look into Henry's face.

"You realize I've lived a long, fulfilled life and enjoyed my wonderful family whom I love. You know that don't you?" Her mother's voice was strong and sure.

"Yes, Mom." She placed her hand over her heart. "And we love you. We'll take care of you. Don't go." She sobbed the words as tears blinded her eyes.

Her mother moved close to Lauren, their faces level with each other. "Yes, I know you all are here to take care of me, but I can't live like this anymore. It's too painful to be so helpless and confused all the time. I won't do it any longer." She took Lauren's hand in hers. "I hope you understand. I don't want to live like this anymore. It's time to go, and Henry is here to escort me."

Her mother encircled her with her arms, her love blanketing her with comfort. Holding her tightly, Lauren did not want to let go, but her mother gently lifted Lauren's arms and stepped back to Henry's side.

Henry's arms opened wide with his palms up. "I wish it could have been different. I wish I had more time on Earth with you. But, I've been by your side all these years watching you take your first steps, your first day of school, graduations."

"And you were there with me when I got the news that Brandon died, weren't you?"

He nodded his head. "Yes, I was."

"I felt comfort one night when I received a message in a dream that Brandon was okay and he was happy." Her eyes puddled with tears. "You were the messenger from him, weren't you?"

"Indeed I was and so happy I could at least do that much for you, my beautiful daughter."

"Why didn't I see you until now?"

"You weren't ready. You weren't open to seeing me until now." His sonorous voice soothed her as he approached her.

Lauren tried to resist. She wanted to be angry with him, but his beckoning eyes drew her into his arms.

"Take care of her, Henry," she said as she warmed in his embrace. "That's why you were here isn't it? To take her away with you when she was ready to cross over?" She gazed up into his face.

"Yes." He nodded and squeezed her shoulders, then stepped back and held her at arm's length. "Your mother couldn't leave without telling you the truth. I wanted to be here to support both you and your mother and to help her make this transition." Henry returned to Barbara's side.

Lauren's hands fell to her sides as she stared at the young couple standing in front of her. The disbelief and anxiety flowed from her body like an icy stream melting in the spring sunshine. Her mother leaned toward her and blew a last kiss. The shimmering figures disappeared across a threshold to another time.

Chapter Twenty-Four

After the portal to the new dimension closed, Lauren collapsed on the floor sobbing, her heart breaking. She crossed her arms across her middle and pushed as if she could squeeze the grief out of her body. Shuddering uncontrollably, she lay down on the cool floor and let the tears flow down her cheeks.

When she opened her clenched fist, the golden heart glinted in the light.

Rolling her arm across her eyes and nose to swipe away the tears, she glanced up to the bed. The startling sight of her mother's body lying on the bed brought her back to reality. Lauren couldn't gather enough strength to get up.

The door opened and a nurse appeared in the doorway. She rushed to Lauren's side. "Are you okay?" She touched the side of Lauren's neck to check her pulse, but Lauren brushed her aside.

"It's Mom. It's my mother." She pointed to the still form on the bed.

The nurse jumped up, raced to the bed, and pushed the call button for help.

Medical staff raced through the doorway and swarmed around her mother's bed. A nurse helped Lauren to her feet and settled her into the chair at the back of the room.

After a few minutes, the nurse approached Lauren. Her eyes told her what she already knew. "I'm sorry. Your mother's gone." She touched Lauren's shoulder. "We can notify your family."

Lauren looked into the woman's kind face. How difficult it must be to have to tell someone their loved one died.

"No, thank you. I can tell my dad she has passed away." Her throat closed on the words because saying it out loud made it real.

She pulled herself out of the chair to walk to her mother's side. The staff moved away from the bed. Lauren held her mother's hand and smiled when she saw the peaceful expression on her face and gave her one last kiss on the cheek.

"I'll go get my dad and brother and we'll be back." She looked around the room at the attending staff. "Thank you."

* * *

Lauren sat in her car outside the nursing home. The parking lot lights illuminated the heart necklace in the palm of her hand enough to make the diamonds sparkle. She squeezed her hand tightly around it, barely feeling the delicate necklace in her hand. Somehow holding onto it helped her realize the heart was evidence she wasn't dreaming about her mother and Henry.

She took a deep breath and fastened the necklace around her neck. She had to face the truth. Her mother loved both Henry and her dad. She wanted to believe that.

Lauren shook her head to help clear her thoughts. Gathering her strength to face her father with the news of her mother's death, she tried but couldn't erase the memory of her beautiful mother and Henry standing together. She would never forget that moment.

She sat behind the steering wheel with tears streaming down her cheeks. She drew in a ragged breath and wiped the tears from her eyes.

Should she call Randy to meet her at the house? Randy. She shook her head with disappointment when she thought of Randy's part in helping Emmett to sell pot. Her eyes popped open. What if Randy wasn't helping Emmett, but rather Emmett was working for him? Squeezing her eyes closed didn't obliterate that thought from her over-taxed brain.

Picking up her bag to reach for a stray cigarette, she threw it back down on the seat and turned the key in the ignition. Take it one step at a time, she thought. First, she had to tell her dad without Randy's help. She didn't think she could be civil to him at this moment.

As Lauren backed out of the parking space, her cell phone rang. It was one o'clock in the morning. What in the world?

She braked quickly and answered the cell phone.

"Emmett, what are you thinking?

168

"Hello Lauren. Sorry, but Randy asked me to call you. It's your dad. Randy wants you to come over to the funeral home right now. Hurry."

"What happened? Emmett?" The phone disconnected.

She threw the phone down in the passenger seat and guided the car out of the lot. Her heart thundered in her chest and the jackhammer in her head rattled her skull.

She had to calm down. She didn't want to be in an accident. Her hands trembled on the steering wheel as she turned out onto the street. Accident or not, she stomped on the accelerator to get to her father as fast as she could.

* * *

Lauren pulled her key from the ignition, looked for the house key on the key remote, and raced to the back door. Randy hadn't left the porch light on for her. How would she find the keyhole without a light? She checked the door knob. Thank goodness Randy left the door unlocked. She pushed open the door and flipped on the light in the back room.

"Daddy," she cried. Her father sat on a folding chair, his hands behind his back, and a rope wrapped around him several times, tying him to the chair. His tie was tied across his mouth as a gag.

"Welcome, Lauren, to our "tie one on party." A sinister cackle came from behind her.

She pulled her gaze from her dad to see Emmett walking out from behind the opened door with a pistol in his hand. Lauren froze with her keys in her hand.

"Emmett?" Her mind couldn't register what was happening. Her knees buckled from the shock of seeing her father tied to the chair and Emmett standing with a gun.

Emmett grabbed her before she fell to the floor. Pulling her up to his chest, he wrapped his arm around her and crushed her to his chest. She tried to push away from him, but he wouldn't release his grip on her.

"Let me go, Emmett." She wriggled in his grasp. "What did you do to my dad?"

"He's fine, Lauren. We're waiting for you."

Lauren felt scared and helpless. Emmett held her tightly and glared at her.

Was he high on drugs or were these the true eyes of Emmett, the eyes of a killer?

Moving the keys in her hand at her side, she felt for the longest one and pressed it between her thumb and fingers.

Her father wriggled his jaw around and loosened the tie from his mouth. "Lauren, don't fight him. He's crazy."

"Shut up, old man. Lauren won't fight me. She loves me, don't ya', Lauren?" He squeezed her tighter to him, grinding his crotch against her. Bile rose in her throat, but she swallowed it back

"Let me go. You're hurting me." She stopped struggling to break his hold on her and faced Emmett squarely, eye to eye. He was the same height and probably weighed less than she did, but he was strong.

His maniacal smile sparked chills through her body, but she didn't drop her gaze from his face. He relaxed his hold on her. Taking advantage of the opportunity, she whipped her hand up with the key and scratched the jagged key across his face. He screamed and threw her to the floor.

When he pressed his hand to his bleeding cheek, Lauren hurled herself at his legs. Emmett fell hard and the pistol skittered away from him. She darted for the pistol, but Emmett scrambled on top of her. He twisted her wrist practically breaking it in two and grabbed the gun away from her.

Emmett sprang up and stood over her with the pistol aimed at her heart. He gasped for air. Blood streamed through his fingers as he clamped his hand to his face. "You're a dead woman," he said through clenched teeth. His eyes bored through her chest.

She put her hands up in defeat and tried to catch her breath.

"What do you want, Emmett? What are you doing here?" Lauren sat up straighter with her hands in the air as he moved away from her feet and circled behind her.

"I got a debt to collect, and you're going to help me." Holding the gun to the back of her head, he bent over close to her and whispered, "You and your boyfriend Chip.

171

Think you're so high and mighty. Chip's got his balls in a vice------ He owes a lot of money. He didn't get the hint when we took out Tony."

Lauren's stomach turned over.

"You were the one who killed Tony?" Lauren's face crumpled. "Why?" She couldn't wrap her mind around Emmett murdering Tony.

"He owed the syndicate big time too. They were sending a message, sweet Lauren. Sending a message to your boyfriend," he sneered. If he didn't pay up his fifty thousand dollars to the casino, you would be the next one with a bullet in your brain."

Lauren blinked in disbelief. She refused to even consider such a ridiculous notion.

"Emmett. Listen to me," Jensen wriggled in his chair. "If it's money you want, I'll give it to you. We can go to the bank when it opens this morning."

"Oh no, sir, I ain't the one he owes the money to. It's the big boys who own the casino, the Detroit syndicate." Glancing back at Lauren, he said, "You have to call Chip and give him the message that you're right here and will be dead if he doesn't pay up." He smiled so wide, Lauren could see all the teeth in his mouth.

Gathering her wits about her, Lauren remembered the conversation with Chip. He was stealing money from the farm to pay his debt. Did he do it to save her life? Tears sprang from her eyes and down her cheek.

"But if I pay his debt to the guys, they wouldn't care. They want the money, right?" Jensen's eyes flashed in anger.

"Shut up." Emmett waved his gun at Lauren's dad.

Jensen shook his head. "What'd they do? Threaten you they'd cut off your drug supply? They bullied you into killing a good man like Tony."

"Well, excuse me, Big Shot. You don't know shit."

The back door banged shut and then opened and shut keeping up a jarring rhythm with its openings and closings. The light in the ceiling popped allowing only the street light through the windows to illuminate the room. Cold air sent goose bumps up and down Lauren's arms and her teeth chattered like it was a January freeze, not the middle of the summer.

"What the hell?" Emmett's eyes grew large. "What's going on?" Pictures flew off the walls pummeling Emmett with broken glass and shards of wood. The whirlwind lashed against him throwing him against the wall. Emmett screamed in terror. "Stop it. Stop it." Dropping his pistol in the middle of the room, he scrambled out the door and down the steps.

Silence followed. Jensen and Lauren sat in mute amazement. "Sweet Jesus. What was that?" Jensen's pale face scared Lauren. "I can't explain what happened, but I'm glad it did."

"I hope it was just a dream, Dad." She quickly jumped up and locked the door. She moved toward her father and tugged at the ropes. "I need to call the police."

"Lauren, no. Emmett's not going to return here again after what he experienced tonight, you can bet on that." A wicked grin spread across Jensen's face.

Jensen stood up and turned around for her to release the plastic bands around his wrist. "Grab my pocket knife and cut these off."

"Emmett almost killed us and admitted he murdered Tony." Lauren quickly found the knife and removed the bloody bands from his bleeding wrists. She pulled his clean white handkerchief from his back pocket and handed it to him when she turned him around to face her. He wiped the blood away, the crimson spots staining the handkerchief. Lauren blinked away from the stark sight.

"So we let Emmett run away and do whatever he wants to do?" She leaned in toward her father. "The police need to find him. He's crazy. He's a murderer. He'll come back to get us and kill Chip too." She could hear her voice almost shrieking at her father.

Jensen lightly gripped Lauren's arms and held her as his sincere eyes pierced through her fear. "If we call the police, Randy and Emmett are dead men."

Chapter Twenty-Five

Lauren backed away from her father, her hands covering her mouth to squelch the gasp of disbelief. Her voice tinged with anger, she said, "Dad, you can't tell me Randy and Emmett are dead men and then drop it. Emmett didn't threaten Randy. He was going to kill me!" She pointed to her chest as she finished her rant. She couldn't stop the trembling coursing its way through her body as she waited for her father to explain himself. Was her dad aware of Randy and Emmett and their connection with the marijuana?

"Sorry, Lauren. I shouldn't have said that. I was just talking off the top of my head." He glanced away from her and studied his bloody wrists.

"Dad." Her eyes narrowed as she studied her father's face. "Tell me the truth. If you know something I don't, you need to tell me now. What is it?" Her heart thudded in her chest.

Jensen dropped his hands to his sides. Lauren realized how spent he was. His body nearly wilted in front of her.

"I need, we need, to get some rest. Let's figure out how to deal with all of this in the morning. I can't think straight right now," he said.

"Well, if you won't tell me what's going on, I'm calling Gary. He can help us." Her eyes searched the room looking for her purse so she could retrieve her cell phone.

Jensen sighed. "All right. All right, but I need a drink. Let me sit a minute and get myself together. Okay?"

She watched him trudge down the hallway to the family room. How in the world could she tell him that Mom is dead while he is dealing with all of this too? She needed Randy here.

Lauren followed him down the hallway and asked, "Where's Randy? We should call him and let him know what happened."

"He's over at Lindsay's place. He's practically moved in with her now."

How long had it been since she even talked to her brother? She had no idea he was that involved with Lindsay. "What if Emmett is going over to Lindsay's? Her kids. Dad, we've got to call him."

"Yes, go ahead and call Randy. He'll know how to handle Emmett." Jensen collapsed in the chair, wiping his wrists with the handkerchief. "Her number is tacked on the bulletin board in the office." He threw the handkerchief to the floor, put his elbows on his knees, and braced his forehead with his hands.

Lauren looked around the room searching for Henry's shadow. She felt he was there, but he was invisible. *Henry, thank you for saving us from Emmett.* A sudden feeling of warmth and relief washed over her. She caught the flicker of his shadow in the corner of her eye and then it disappeared.

* * *

Randy must have raced over to the funeral home because only minutes elapsed until he charged through the back door as if he were rushing to a fire call. Lauren met him in the hallway.

"How's Dad?" His eyes were filled with concern as the siblings stood together in the hall.

"He's okay. Resting in the family room. He's exhausted. I just made coffee for him to help perk him up a bit." Lauren's eyes filled with tears. "Oh, Randy."

Her mother's death and the terror of the last hour overcame Lauren. She couldn't stop the sobs and the tears tracing down her cheeks. Feeling safe with Randy at her side, she finally allowed herself to let go of her fear and anger and allow the grief to overcome her.

He pulled his handkerchief from his back pocket and handed it to her. "Hey, Sis. It's going to be okay." She rubbed tears from her eyes and wiped her nose. She wadded the handkerchief up in her fist to hand it back to him. "Thanks," she said.

Randy waved it away. "No, no. You can keep it."

He turned away from her to find his dad, but Lauren grabbed his arm and moved in front of him. "Wait a minute. I have something to tell you before you go in there."

She focused her gaze on his eyes. "Mom passed away tonight."

His eyes clouded as he processed her statement. His face crumpled. "No." She pulled his slack body into her arms. Time seemed to stop in the crushing silence.

"We have to tell Dad, but I don't know if he can handle it right now." She stepped away from him and dabbed her eyes and nose with the damp handkerchief, thankful he had refused to take it back.

"All right." He sucked in a deep breath "We'll wait until we can sort out Emmett's situation. We have to take care of the living first." He pulled her to his side in a one-armed hug as he walked her to the family room where their father waited for them.

Randy escorted Lauren to the chair and sat next to their dad on the couch, closer than usual.

"How ya' doin', Dad?" Randy patted his father's leg and sat back in the couch.

Lauren watched her brother and father from where she sat in the wing-backed chair next to the couch. She loved these two men. She vowed she would do anything possible to protect them, but how could she if she didn't know the truth about Emmett and Randy. She hesitated to ask questions when she saw her father's pale face.

But if Emmett was to be stopped, she had to convince them to call the police.

"I told you on the phone Emmett killed Tony. He's crazy. He was going to kill us if I couldn't find Chip. We have to call the police. He's not in his right mind." Lauren twisted the damp handkerchief.

Randy shifted his glance at his sister to his father. "What did you tell her, Dad?"

"Nothing." Jensen shook his head and sighed.

Lauren scooted toward the front of the chair and leaned toward Randy. "Tell me, Randy. What's going on?"

Chapter Twenty-Six

"I'm sorry, Lauren. I'm truly sorry." Randy sat up straight, then stood up and began pacing.

"What are you hiding from me?"

Randy stopped behind the couch. "A few weeks ago Emmett asked me to help him out. He was in a bind. His boss told him the storage for the pot drop-off had been compromised. The police were onto them about the location. His boss told Emmett to find another place to hide it."

Lauren's eyes opened wide with the realization. "His boss? You mean the criminal behind the drug ring, don't you?"

Randy shrugged. "Yeah, okay."

"So you told him he could use the funeral home as a warehouse for the drugs?"

"Yeah, and I'm not proud of it. But Emmett would be in big trouble if he couldn't find a place right away."

Lauren folded her arms and frowned as she waited for the next revelation,

"Don't look at me like that. Emmett's been a good buddy to me for most of my life." He frowned back at Lauren, dropped his gaze to the floor, and then faced her again with a grim expression. "So I told him okay. He could stash it here for a couple of weeks till he made arrangements for another place," Randy said in a hard tone of voice. "No, no, don't lecture me. Dad's already done that. I don't need any more from you."

Lauren whirled toward her father. "You knew about this? You said okay to stashing weed here?" Her palm slapped her forehead. "Unbelievable."

Randy jumped in before Jensen had a chance to respond. "Dad found the stuff. I didn't ask him, Lauren."

"Oh, please, Randy. So helping a friend is your explanation for committing a crime, for involving your whole family in this ridiculous, but deadly situation." She ground her fists into her thighs trying not to give into the urge to pummel her brother till he told her the truth.

Randy cocked his eyebrow. "That's all I'm saying. Please believe me."

"So now, since Tony was murdered in our garage and the police are watching this place, he can't move the stuff out of here. Right?" Lauren's eyes blazed with anger.

"Yeah, you've got that right." Randy leaned back in the couch.

"If we call the cops, Randy and Emmett will be walking around with a target on their backs. The syndicate doesn't want any witnesses to their drug operation talking to the police." Jensen threw up his hands and shook his head. "We don't have any good options here."

Lauren shot up out of her chair. "Damn it, Randy. What in the world were you thinking?" Her voice was an octave higher than normal. "Of all the ridiculous things you've done, this is the most thoughtless and stupid." She flopped back into the chair like a rag doll. "I don't get it."

Taking a deep breath she said, "So you're saying, you tried to help Emmett out of a jam, and now he wants to kill me?" She formed her fingers into a gun and pointed it at her head. "Thanks so much, dear brother." Her voice coated with sarcasm.

"The way I figure it, Emmett's boss told him to come after you in order to flush Chip out. Kind of like hold you for ransom till Chip pays off his gambling debt." Randy said. "And Chip knows they would do it because they ordered Tony killed for not paying off his debt."

Randy shook his head. "I'm surprised they didn't shoot Chip. But, then they'd never get the debt paid."

"That must be why someone ran Chip off the road near Jenkins Creek. Trying to scare him." Lauren looked up at Randy to see if he agreed. "You suspected that didn't you?"

Randy hesitated. "Yeah. I kind of put it together like that."

"Jenkins Creek?" Jensen straightened up. "When did that happen?"

"A couple of days ago. I haven't seen or heard from Chip since. He could be in Mexico by now," Lauren said.

Lauren's eyes drilled into Randy. "Emmett is some good friend to you and Chip, eh, Randy?" She scowled as she said, "And he killed our friend, Tony." Her voice choked.

"Emmett told us he killed Tony as a message to jolt Chip into paying his debt." Lauren shook her head. "Someone must have bullied Emmett to turn him into a murderer."

"Emmett's hooked on drugs. I'm sure they threatened to cut him out of the drug deals or kill him if he didn't do what they ask," Randy said. "I'm afraid for both Emmett and Chip."

"You don't have to worry about Chip, kids. The syndicate won't kill him."

Randy and Lauren turned toward their father. "Why would you say that," Lauren asked.

Jensen blinked. "I know Chip. That's all." He stretched his hands over his head and yawned. "I'm going to bed. You both stay here tonight. I don't want Lauren alone at her duplex."

Jensen looked at Lauren whose lips were curled and ready to speak. "No, Sis, no more. I've had it for the night, or should I say for the morning? I'm done. Go to bed." He stood up from the couch. "Make a note, will ya'? We need a new davenport to replace this one. Damn thing is so uncomfortable."

"Dad, wait." Lauren flashed a glance at Randy. He nodded his head. "Sit down a minute. We have something to tell you."

"I don't want to hear any more about drugs or Emmett. I'm sick of all of it."

Randy walked over and faced him. "Please, Dad, sit down. We aren't talking about that. It's about Mom."

Chapter Twenty-Seven

Later that morning the sun's rays exploded through the open blinds of the windows in the family room where Lauren crashed after raiding the liquor cabinet with her brother. The dazzle penetrated through her eye lids and right into her brain. She slashed her hand through the air and pressed it down over her aching eyes. Sitting up on the couch, she turned her back to the sun's rays, and pressed her hands hard against her temples. The room tilted and blurred. Blinking away the fuzzy view, she sat frozen in place, afraid to move her head for fear it might fall off. Her stomach flipped over a few times and she knew she was going to be sick. Lauren stumbled as fast as she could to the half-bath off the family room making it just in time to hurl into the toilet.

"Hey, Sis. You're looking fine this morning." Randy smirked at her from the bathroom doorway.

"Don't talk to me." She clutched the rim of the toilet and eased her body down to the floor, but not loosening her grip on the toilet. She knew she was going to need it again soon.

"I've got the coffee ready out here. Didn't figure you'd feel like climbing the steps to the kitchen upstairs." He winked and sauntered away from the door. She would've thrown the toilet brush at him if she had the strength to do so.

* * *

Walking back into the family room, the cold tile on her bare feet felt good. She was so hot and sweaty. She grabbed a bottle of cold water from the small refrigerator under the counter and guzzled it down.

"You should've been drinking water early this morning instead of a constant stream of rum and Coke, eh?" He stood next to her. His eyes softened with concern. "You want some coffee?"

She brushed her hair away from her face and nodded. Randy set the mug on the counter for her. Lauren turned away and flopped into the chair that faced away from the sunny windows.

"Um, here ya' go. You forgot your coffee." He leaned down and gave her the cup, not removing his hand from the mug until she had a firm grasp on it. Randy pulled the drapes closed to block out some of the morning sun.

One little sip before she placed the cup on her thigh. She rested her elbow on the arm of the chair and held her head with her free hand. Miserable was the only word that could describe her this morning.

"Where's Dad," she asked.

"Dad just got back with Mom." His voice choked.

Her head popped up. "Is he okay?"

"I guess so. I asked him if he wanted me to call Swartz to take care of her, but he said no." His hands to his side, he said, "Dad told me no one would take the time to care for her like he would." He frowned. "He doesn't even want me in the prep room with him. He's going to call Norma to do her make-up and hair. He trusts her." He stared at the floor.

Lauren blinked back her tears. Reality. Loss even comes to the family of the funeral director. "That's how much he loves her, huh, Randy. This will be the last act of love he can do for her."

"Yeah, I guess." He swiped at his eyes. "How're you doing? Can I get you anything?"

Lauren rubbed her forehead. "How about a couple of aspirin out of the drawer by the sink? It feels like someone is clanking bowling balls in my skull."

Randy opened the drawer and fished around a bit till he retrieved the aspirin. "Here you go," he said as he delivered them and a glass of water to his sister.

"I'm going to check on Dad. Then run over to Lindsay's and tell her about Mom."

"Wait a minute. We need to figure out what to do about Emmett. What about Chip? I mean, come on, Randy."

Randy dropped to one knee. He held Lauren's shoulders and caught her gaze with his. "I'm sorry, Sis. Are you afraid? I won't leave you if you are." Lauren choked up when she saw her brother's troubled eyes.

"No, I'm not afraid. I just feel so helpless. I want to help Chip. I want Emmett to get some help. I know once he comes down from that murderous high, he'll need someone with him." She leaned closer to Randy.

"You need to find him. You guys need to end this ridiculous charade and admit to the police what you've done. Emmett can help the police bust the drug ring. If you go in, it'll be better for you."

Lauren touched Randy's hands on her shoulders. "Please, Randy. Stop this madness now. I'm so afraid what might happen to you. Please."

"Okay. I have to go. I have to take care of a few things," he said softly.

She held onto his hands. The knot in her throat blocked off any more words.

"I'll be careful." He pulled his hands away from her and stood up. "I'll be fine. You stay here and keep the doors locked. Check on Dad pretty soon, okay?"

Randy turned and walked out of the family room. When she heard the back door shut, Lauren bawled. She heard the cries and wailing. When she took a breath, she realized those sounds were coming from her, from the depths of her. She slid out of the upholstered chair to the soft rug on the floor. She lay on her side, curled up into the fetal position, and sobbed.

Chapter Twenty-Eight

Lauren dried her hair with a luxurious, fluffy towel that made her think of a fancy hotel instead of her father's shower. After a nap and the shower, she felt almost human again. She tossed her hair back and finger-combed it as she studied herself in the mirror. Her eyes weren't exactly sparkling back at her, and physically she felt stronger, but there was a gaping hole in her heart with the loss of her mother.

She hung the towel on the rack and slipped into the shorts and tee shirt she found in her antique chest of drawers in her old room upstairs. Thankfully there were no funeral services today or grieving families to meet, so comfy clothes were appropriate and preferred.

Her stomach growled with hunger. No wonder. When she slipped on her watch, she noted it was past lunch time. Placing her hand on her stomach didn't stop the growling.

On her way to the kitchen, she noticed Randy's bedroom door was ajar. She started to tap on the door, but decided she didn't want to wake him if he were napping. She peeked around the door, but no Randy in the unmade bed. She shook her head at the clothing dropped on the floor and chair. Looked like the room she remembered when he was in middle school.

Except now the bedroom was equipped with a laptop and electronics any techno-geek would desire. She walked over to his desk and eyed the desktop computer, external drive, and extra screen. He must be using his money wisely to afford all this plus the ginormous TV screen that dwarfed one bedroom wall.

Closing the door behind her, she steeled herself not to go back into Randy's room and straighten up the mess because she knew he wouldn't appreciate her doing it. She smiled when she remembered his sign on his door when they were kids. "No girls allowed."

Where was he? She shook her head. Hopefully, he was with Emmett and figuring out a solution to Emmett's troubling situation.

Lauren headed for the apartment kitchen. She turned to the open stairwell when she heard the doorbell ring. "Dad? Can you answer the door?" She winced at the thought of greeting a family in her shorts and tank top.

Lauren could hear her father talking to a man, but the voices were muffled. She made her way to the kitchen trying not to notice the sink full of dishes begging her to load them into the dishwasher.

"Lauren, come on down. Gary's here to see us." Her dad's voice echoed up the stairwell.

Gary was here. Her heart skittered a bit. Her head was wet and she had no make-up on. *Get ahold of yourself, girl*. He's not here for a date, but wouldn't that be great if he were here to take her away for a beautiful drive together to the lake and a romantic afternoon at the beach?

She scowled wondering exactly what the nature of his visit could be. Emmett? Randy? Chip? Did he know Randy was hiding drugs in the funeral home?

Lauren rushed down the steps. Her eyes sparkled when she saw Gary waiting in the foyer, so handsome in his uniform. She couldn't stop the grin from spreading across her face as she glimpsed him sweeping her body with his gaze and checking out her bare legs.

"Good morning." She met his look as she walked toward him. The connection was so strong she could barely stop herself from embracing him.

"I think you mean good afternoon, Lauren," her dad corrected her.

"Oh, yeah, I guess you're right." She didn't drop her eyes from Gary's face.

He twirled his police officer hat in his hands. "Hi, Lauren." His voice was all business and the pleasant look on his face from earlier had disappeared.

"I wonder if we might sit down and talk for a minute?" He motioned toward the family room. Her dad walked ahead of them, and she and Gary followed. Being next to him sent warm sensations tickling up and down her arms and legs.

"You'd better take a seat in the chair, Gary. That couch is damn uncomfortable," Jensen said.

"Thanks, but I can't stay." He waited as Lauren slid onto the couch and her dad took the wing-backed chair. "Well, okay," he said as he eased his large frame onto the cushion next to Lauren.

"I'm sorry to hear about your wife." His eyes swung over to Lauren, "And your mother." He put his arm around her shoulders and squeezed. "If there's anything I can do to help you out in the next few days, please let me know."

"Thank you. I appreciate that very much." Jensen cleared his throat.

Lauren nodded and tried to be brave, but it was difficult with Gary sitting close to her with his arm around her. She wanted to hide away from the reality of her mother's death.

He slid his hand down Lauren's arm and clenched her hand in his.

The ringing phone in the office interrupted his sentence.

"Excuse me, Gary. I better get that." Jensen rose and left the room to answer the phone.

"So what's up? Can you stay for coffee?" She smiled. "Oh, that's right, you don't drink coffee." Lauren's eyes twinkled with an impish gleam.

The policeman grinned. "You got that right."

He shook his head. "I'm sorry I'm not here for coffee. I came over to tell you in person before you got the call." He cleared his throat. "It's about Emmett."

192

"Oh, did Randy talk to you about Emmett?" Her heart jumped hoping that Randy had actually gone to the police.

"No, I haven't seen Randy." His brows knitted together. "Was he looking for me?"

"Oh, well, uh." She looked past Gary not wanting to face him while trying to conjure up a cover story for letting it slip that Randy might have been looking for him. She licked her lips.

Jensen appeared at the doorway. "The phone call was from the M.E.'s office." His slack-jawed expression and pale face frightened Lauren. "Emmett's family wants us to handle the arrangements for his funeral."

Chapter Twenty-Nine

Lauren's brain refused to accept the reality that Emmett was dead. The thought threw her world into turmoil. She leaped off the couch, pushing her fist into her stomach to try and settle the roiling in her belly.

"You said they called for arrangements for Emmett's funeral?" She caught her father's gaze willing him not to confirm the horrible news.

"I'm sorry, Lauren. Emmett is dead." Jensen pulled his hand across his face.

Rising from the couch, Gary placed his arm around her shoulders and she collapsed onto his chest. Jensen dropped into the chair across from them.

Tipping Lauren's chin up to face her, Gary said, "That's what I was going to tell you. Emmett was found dead in his car this morning by a passing motorist on Jenkins Creek Road." She shook her head not wanting to believe it.

"What happened? How did he die?" Randy's husky voice jarred them. He stood in the doorway with fists clenched to his sides.

"We don't know for sure yet. The autopsy will be performed tomorrow," Gary said.

"Well you must have some idea. Were you there at the scene?" Randy leaned forward waiting for the answers.

"Yes, I was there, but you know I can't say anything."

"Don't play the cop card now, Gary. We're all friends. Tell us what happened to Emmett." He took a step closer to Gary.

"It looks like suicide. Gunshot to the head." Gary glanced down to the floor before returning to face Randy. "You'll know anyway when you see his body."

"Oh, my God. I knew he was out of his mind last night. He had to be."

Gary grasped Lauren's hand. "Did you see him last night?"

"Yes. He was here."

"Lauren." Randy cautioned, slightly moving his head from side to side.

"So how was his state of mind when you saw him?"

Lauren dropped her eyes from Randy. She faced Gary. "He was very agitated. I think he was high on something."

Jensen stood up. "Thanks for trying to prepare us for the news. I think we need some time to accept this. Will you leave now so Lauren can rest?"

"I'm fine, Dad. I'm no wilting violet. I'm fine."

"All right, Mr. Staab. When I find out more, I'll be back later." He offered his hand for a handshake and Jensen returned the offer by grasping Gary's hand and covering it with his other one.

Gary turned to Lauren and gave her a quick hug. "I'll talk with you soon," he said in a voiced choked with emotion.

When the front door closed, the three remained silent in the room.

"I searched everywhere I could think of to find him." Randy covered his face with his hands and pressed them hard into his eyes. Sucking in a ragged breath, he looked at Lauren. "If only I would have begun searching last night instead of staying here trying to drink away my troubles." His eyes glistened with moisture. "I could've saved Emmett."

Jensen hugged Randy as if he were comforting him after he'd crashed his bike when he was six years old. Lauren joined the two of them and they all stood together in a group hug.

Randy's humming phone broke up the embrace as he pulled it from the holster on his belt. "Yeah. Okay. I'll meet you there. You heard about Emmett? Okay."

Slipping his phone in his pocket, Randy said, "I've got to go."

"Was that Chip," Lauren asked.

"No, it was Lindsey." Randy didn't look at Lauren. "Dad, you'll be okay?"

"Oh, sure, go ahead."

"I'm going with you." Lauren announced.

"You don't need to go. Lindsey just needs something."

"Oh really?" Lauren's voice filled with cynicism.

Randy turned away from her and strode out the door. Lauren scampered to catch up with him at the back door. "Randy, you're going to meet Chip, and I'm going with you."

"No, you're not." He pushed her away from him.

"Randy, you take me with you or I'm going to the police and tell them what happened last night," her voice hissed in his ear.

He whirled around to face her. His eyes shot bolts of anger at her, but she didn't back down.

"You would too, wouldn't you?" He smiled faintly. "Okay, Sis. You're in. Come on."

Chapter Thirty

Lauren and Randy jumped into Randy's Jeep parked in the funeral home parking lot. He pressed the pedal down hard and they squealed out of the parking space.

"Where are we going to meet Chip?" Lauren asked clinging to the dashboard of the car as he swung the vehicle onto Main Street. Randy's driving when he was mad scared her, but she was determined to see Chip and Randy was her ticket to meet him. She couldn't wait to confront him and give him a piece of her mind.

"You'll see," Randy said in a dismissive tone. He drove the streets in town edging over the speed limit, but as soon as they hit the blacktop toward Chip's farm, he pushed the Jeep to its full speed. Lauren tested her seat belt to make sure she was clicked in. She bit her lip to refrain from asking more questions. Talking to him would only aggravate him and distract him from his already risky driving.

Speeding past the driveway to Chip's farm, Randy steered the Jeep onto a dirt lane about a mile beyond the farm. He geared down the motor so their teeth wouldn't clatter as they rumbled over the ruts and holes in the roadway.

Lauren recalled fun memories of two-tracking down the bumpy road. She and Chip had their own style of carnival ride as they jounced down the lane. After a rain it was even more exciting with mud flying up on the bumpers and sides and covering the windshield.

Looking at the dark clouds gathering in the south, she wondered if it would be raining when they rode back home and doubted there would be any element of fun in that trip. What could Randy possibly say to Chip? She winced, thinking the only way to save herself and Chip was for her dad to give the money to Chip to pay off the gambling debt.

As they continued, the thick woods on each side gave way to an intersection. Randy turned right on a gravel road not any smoother than the lane they had traversed, and quickly turned left into an old homestead. The house and outbuildings had been leveled by a tornado years ago, but the old abandoned barn remained at the back of the property. Hidden by overgrown bushes and trees, the once red wooden barn was now a faded, peeling hulk.

When they approached the barn, Lauren spotted Chip's truck parked out front. She glanced over at her brother. His sober face clued her in to his dark mood. He parked next to Chip's truck and turned off the ignition. "You wait here."

"I didn't ride out here with you to sit in the Jeep. I'm going in to talk to Chip. I have plenty I want to say to him." She grabbed for the door handle, but Randy's hand clutched her shoulder as if it were in a vise.

"You're staying here," he commanded.

She tried to pull away from his painful grasp, but it was no use. "Let go. You're hurting my shoulder."

He loosened his grip. His narrowed eyes and creased brow scared her.

"I mean it, Lauren. You stay here till I tell you to come in."

"And when will that be—when hell freezes over?" She felt the vise clamp back down on her shoulder. "Okay, okay. I get it. Let go." He made her feel like the bratty little sister who used to torment her big brother by taking away one of his Legos. Today the stakes were much higher than a stolen Lego.

Randy let go of her and slid out of the vehicle in one smooth movement. Lauren grimaced in pain as she rubbed her shoulder and made a few circular movements with it. At least, it still worked.

Randy strode up the wide berm leading to the large entrance that accommodated the entry of giant-sized farm machinery into the aged building. The doors were pushed back in their rusty tracks revealing what looked like the opening to a black tomb. He disappeared inside the vast darkness.

Lauren's knee bounced as she waited and watched the doorway for signs of Chip or Randy. She swiped her hand across her sweaty forehead. The air was thick with heat and humidity. Perspiration puddled in her armpits, but it wasn't from the weather, rather from her raw nerves. Her heart pounded in her chest fearing what might be happening inside.

She could wait no longer. She quietly opened the car door, slipped out and turned to close the door but not latch it so they wouldn't hear her. Using the back of the truck and Jeep as a screen between her and the barn, she ducked low and ran parallel to the front of the building far enough so she could sneak up toward the barn without being seen from the entrance.

Sprinkles of rain fell on her shoulders and hair as she crept along the outside wall toward the doorway, listening and praying they wouldn't know she was closing in. The need to hear what they were discussing drove her to become bolder. Her feet carried her near to the huge open doorway. Randy and Chip's loud voices reverberated through the opening.

"It's got to stop now, Chip. The syndicate is going to hunt us down. You know it. I know it." Randy's angry voice echoed off the old barn walls.

"You know my dad isn't going to let his friends take me out. Sure we've kind of diverted the drug sales to our pockets and claimed a few of their customers. But, my dad's been doing business with them for years. Maybe they'll slap our hands, but that's it." Chip moderated his voice. "Come on, Randy."

Drug sales? Chip's dad? She flinched. Her eyes widened with this shocking news.

Fearing her breathing might be heard, she gulped a breath and flattened her body against the door of the barn. She inched her way to the barn's entranceway. Raindrops splattered in her face.

"No. You don't get it. I want out now." Randy said, his voice strained with anger.

Lauren clasped her hand over her mouth to stifle a cry. Her mind whirled with the idea of her brother involved in drug deals with Chip. How could he be so stupid?

"Tony's dead. They killed him! These guys don't just slap your hands." Randy stopped to take a breath. "For God's sake, Emmett's dead!"

Lauren peeked around the door far enough to get one eye on the angry men.

"The business is spinning out of control. No more drug sales. You don't need to grow anymore weed to supply those sales. I'm done with it." He flung his arms across his body like he was calling Chip safe at first base. But they were not playing a kid's game now.

"You can't quit. You know too much about the operations. I can't let you quit." Chip stepped closer to Randy. "You should've known that when you said okay to get in on the deal. We aren't playing games here." Chip pulled a handgun concealed in his waistband and pointed it at Randy.

Lauren's heart raced, actually feeling the rapid pulse in her neck. She had to do something quick.

"Oh, so this is the way it's going to end between friends. My best friend Chip." His voice filled with sarcasm. Randy lowered his voice. "Put the gun down."

Chip cocked the gun and aimed it at Randy's heart. Randy held his hands up in the air.

Lauren sprang into the doorway. "Stop it, Chip." She yelled so loud she thought she broke her vocal cords.

When Chip swung the gun toward Lauren, Randy slammed his body full force onto Chip's legs knocking him down to the wooden floor of the barn. The gun flew across the gritty floor and Randy jumped up to grab the weapon before Chip could reach it. Chip tackled Randy bringing him down hard. Both men struggled no longer like school boys in a playground fight, but rather as warriors fighting to the death. Randy was no match for Chip whose high school wrestling skills kicked in.

With heart rattling in her chest, Lauren chased after the gun.

The grunts and groans of the men filled her ears, but she focused on the hand gun. Her mouth and eyes clogged with dust and sand stirred up by the fighters. She blindly dove for the gun and rejoiced when she grasped the hard metal in her hand.

Feeling triumphant, as if she had won a trophy, Lauren jumped up and, using both hands, she aimed the barrel at Chip. "Stop it. Stop it now. I've got the gun," she screamed.

The men continued the battle ignoring her scream. Lauren fired two shots in the air.

Startled by the gunfire, they rolled away from each other and covered their heads with their arms.

Lauren lowered the gun and pointed it at Chip. She rocked back and forth with nervous energy and fear.

"What the hell?" Getting to his feet, Chip bent over propping himself with his hands on his knees. He gulped in deep breaths.

"Well, hey, my little sister has balls, huh, Chip?" Randy managed to say as he gained an upright position. "Give me the gun, Sis." Was that pride she saw flicker across her brother's face?

"Wait a minute. Just a minute." She held up the palm of her hand and glanced back and forth between the two men. She realized she hadn't figured out what to do once she had retrieved the gun. She tried to give the impression she was in control and not let on her knees were so weak she could collapse at any minute.

She wiped away the dirt from her eyes before she continued. Waving her free hand in the air as she talked, "I don't know what all is going on here, but I'm going to call the police." She would be dialing right now if she had her phone, but she hadn't brought her bag with her. "Randy, let me have your phone." She wiggled her fingers toward him to let him know she could hold it in that hand.

"First, give me the gun, Lauren. Then I'll give you the phone." A quick grin flashed toward her. "You know how to get it done, Sis."

She side-stepped over to Randy keeping the gun pointed at Chip. Without taking her eyes off of him, she handed Randy the gun.

"Aw, come on. You know I wouldn't have shot you. You're my friend." Chip's whiny voice grated on her nerves. Lauren wanted to slap his face. Always trying to manipulate people with his sad, sincere-like eyes. No more. She was wise to his ways now. Too late.

"You call the police and we're both going to jail. You know that, don't you? They'll lock us both up. Is that what you want?" Chip's voice oozed with indignation.

Randy pointed the gun at Chip. "I'm willing to take my chances in court. When I testify against you and the whole syndicate, I think I'll get a fair shake."

"You'll be a dead man." The words hit Lauren hard in the gut.

"Shut up. I don't want you to say anything more. I'm sick of you. I should've never listened to you." Randy straightened his back and pulled back his shoulders. "We're calling the cops, and that's it."

With the weapon securely in his hand, he glanced down to pull his phone out of the holster on his belt. Taking advantage of the movement, Chip lunged at Lauren and grabbed her pinning her back to his chest encasing her body with his muscular arms. He held her so tightly she couldn't wriggle away or slide down from his grasp. He was crushing her ribs, so she could barely breathe as she watched her brother's face explode red with anger.

"If you shoot, you'll kill your sister," Chip said through clenched teeth.

"Let her go, Chip. You hurt her and I swear, I'll kill you, you son of a bitch." Randy stood powerless even if he did control the gun.

Chapter Thirty-One

"Get outta the way, Randy. Me and your sister are takin' a ride and you're not invited." Chip, crushing Lauren against his chest with both arms, pulled Lauren toward the door. She tried to resist by mashing Chip's foot or even his toe. With his muscular wrestler's strength, he easily lifted her up and backed toward the doorway, while she flailed her legs with no results.

"Let me go," she screamed wrenching her body to try and break his hold on her.

"Stop, Chip." Randy yelled. His eyes narrowed as he aimed the gun at him.

'You better be sure you can shoot that gun and hit me, otherwise your dear sis is dead." Chip continued moving away from Randy and lugging Lauren toward the wide door.

"Randy, don't shoot." She barely had enough breath to speak. She didn't want to be shot, but more than that, she didn't want Randy to shoot Chip and face charges and the guilt of murdering a friend. A friend? No friend would do this. Her arms and chest ached from the pressure Chip used to clutch her so forcefully

The cold rain shocked her as Chip carted her out of the dusty barn. She tried to fill her compressed lungs with the fresh air willing herself not to black out.

"Don't follow us. He's got a shotgun in his truck." Her breathless voice was barely audible.

Randy stood motionless, holding the gun down to his side. His gaze focused on every step carrying Lauren farther away from him and closer to danger. Chip pulled Lauren down the berm.

"Let her go," Randy yelled from the barn doorway. "I won't shoot." He placed the gun on the barn floor beside him and held his hands over his head.

Lightning split the sky overhead as Lauren watched Randy walk through the doorway and stand in the pouring rain.

"Now, I'd be an idiot to take that deal. You know he'll shoot me as soon as he has a chance," he hissed into Lauren's ear.

"Chip…" The boom of thunder was deafening.

"Shut up. Come along like a good girl and you'll be fine. I'm not going to hurt you."

"You're hurting me now," she managed to breathe out. Rain pummeled her face and wind sent chills through her cold, wet body.

He relaxed his hold on her so at last, she could take a deep breath.

Chip pulled her around to the driver's side of his truck to shield them from Randy. "Get in there and be good." He opened the door and shoved her into the seat. He reached into the back seat of the truck to grab his rifle from the gun rack.

Lauren scooted across the leather driver's seat, dived across the large console and banged against the passenger door. She grabbed the handle and threw herself against the door falling out into the mud. She scrambled away from the truck and began running low to the ground toward Randy. Getting a foothold in the slippery mud and long grass was impossible. The ground came up to meet her as she splayed out flat on the rain soaked earth.

Randy picked up the gun and fired off several rounds as he ran toward Chip, but the bullets pinged off the big truck. Chip sprang into his truck, fired up the engine, turned the vehicle around, and gunned it as he headed down the lane. Randy continued firing the weapon at the truck even though it was out of range.

Dropping the gun to the ground, he ran back to the berm where Lauren had tumbled. He pulled her up and held her upright until she could get her balance. Studying her from the top of her head to her toes, he asked, "Are you okay."

She nodded. "And you?" Instead of answering he shoved her to the barn for shelter from the rain and any bullets Chip could shoot at them. She was shivering so hard from the cold, her teeth chattered. She buckled her arms around her body to stop the shivering and capture some warmth.

Lightning strikes and thunder claps came one right after the other. Peeking out the door to see if Chip was gone, the driving rain blocked the view of the lane, and the trees and brush beyond obstructed any sight of the roadway.

"I'm better now, but you're freezing." He dropped the gun to the floor and pulled her against him to use his body to warm her.

After a minute, he stepped back and held up his index finger. "I have to make a call." Randy pulled his phone from his belt holder and punched 9-1-1 into the phone. He said, "I have an emergency at the old Winters' homestead."

He replaced the phone on his belt and took a deep breath after making the call to report Chip's attempt to kidnap Lauren and using the gun. "I should've called the police a long time ago. Maybe I could've saved Tony and Emmett."

Lauren embraced him. "It's over. I'm fine. You're all right." She rubbed his back to help soothe him. She frowned when she realized, this nightmare wasn't really over. It was just beginning.

Stepping away from him, she said, "What do we do now? Wait here or go to the police station or—." She hesitated. "Or are you going to run?" She faced him now afraid to hear his answer.

"I'm sorry, so sorry." He dropped his head and his shoulders shook from quiet sobs.

"I wish I could rewind the last few months. I never thought any of this would happen." Randy faced her. His eyes glistened. "You've got to believe me, Sis."

"I'm such an idiot. When Chip asked me to join him to form our own drug ring, I only saw the money I could make. He was such a good salesman telling me not to worry about the syndicate bothering us because we were peanuts to them. I wanted to believe I'd make tons of money. Pay off my gambling debts, get a new car, get away from the funeral home." He covered his face with his hands, and then skimmed them through his hair.

Lauren listened but couldn't comprehend her brother was a drug dealer. This picture of her hero, juxtaposed with him as a criminal, seemed like a crazy cartoon drawing. It couldn't be real.

"Wait, wait a minute." She held her hand up toward him. Her glance flashed away from his face and focused on the beams in the ceiling of the barn while she gathered her thoughts.

Levelling her gaze on him, she said, "So you've been lying to us all this time? Making up stories to cover your activities with Chip and Emmett?"

Randy held his hands out to the side as he addressed her. "Yes. I've been lying. Lying so much I'm relieved to know it's over. I got lost in the lies." He shook his head. "I didn't want to hurt anyone. I was crazy to think it was a joy ride and I'd get off when the ride was over."

"But Emmett did get hurt, didn't he?" She got right into his face. "Emmett is dead because of his access to your drugs, but you refused to see Emmett spiraling out of control with his drug addiction."

Randy nodded and lowered his gaze to the ground. "And Tony." he said. An ear-splitting crack of thunder so powerful shook the old barn.

Lauren's hand covered her throat. "No, Randy. No." Her knees buckled and she landed hard on the wooden floor.

Randy squatted down to help Lauren up. "Leave me alone." Her face was twisted in anger. Completely wrung out with no more strength to stand up, she sat up, pulling her knees up to her chest and wrapping her arms tight around her legs. She rocked back and forth on her bottom refusing to look at her brother.

At that moment hatred for her big brother zinged through her body. What was he thinking? Drug deals? His friends dead. Did he murder Tony? Nausea rose in her throat.

"Tony." She searched his face. One part of her wanted to know, but the other part dreaded to find out. "Did you kill Tony?"

"Oh, Lauren. No!" Randy sat down hard on the floor. "I can't believe you think I could do that."

"I can't believe you're a drug dealer, Randy!" she shouted and waved her arms. "Why wouldn't I imagine you as a murderer?"

She watched his face crumple. And she was glad. He had hurt her, her dad, and everyone who knew him with his criminal deeds.

"You have got to believe me, I didn't murder anybody." The cords in his neck tightened as he clenched his jaw.

"Chip thinks they murdered Tony because he was helping Chip. He was in on the growing of the marijuana and actually gathering the drugs to supply the orders." Randy gathered his lanky body into a tight ball matching Lauren. "He believes they left Tony's body in the garage of the funeral home as a warning to Chip that you would be next if he didn't stop the drug deals."

"That plan didn't faze him, did it? We saw how much he cared about me anyway." She squeezed her knees against her chest. "He didn't stop, did he? Is that why he was run off the road? The syndicate wanted to kill him?"

"Oh if they wanted to kill him, they would've. His dad is a big shot in the syndicate. I imagine he ordered someone to scare Chip."

"His own father?" Her eyes grew wide with the realization.

"Yeah. Chip and his dad have had a love-hate relationship all along. Chip was planning to take over eventually and his dad knew it." Randy shook his head. "If anybody else would've tried this, his dad would off them in a second."

Lauren pushed hard on her eyes and forehead with both hands to relieve the pain of the headache flooding her brain. Absorbing the truth was taking its toll on her body. But isn't that what she wanted? To know the truth? Maybe not.

"Chip's dad is a gangster." She almost laughed when she pictured Al DeYoung. He was not a gangster-type guy. He seemed to be a friendly senior citizen when she was around him. The guy that supported the construction of the Little League ball field, the man who passed out candy and money to the kids at Halloween, and the one who kicked in half of the money to build city hall.

"Yeah, you'd never suspect he's the main man here in the west side of the state. Has been for years. He directs and co-ordinates all the drug trafficking around here. You don't mess with Al."

"So Chip has been working for his dad all these years in the drug deals." She could barely choke out this latest revelation. She certainly didn't know Chip at all. What else had he hidden from her?

"Yeah, that's how Chip had all the connections to go in business for himself and cheat the syndicate. In fact Chip was the one with the brilliant idea of growing pot in the cornfields on that huge farm. Money from rows of marijuana hidden among the corn plants helped add even more cash to the syndicate's pockets."

"Chip got greedy and decided to pull in the money for himself and not the syndicate." She remembered the cars, the boats, the electronics, Chip owned over the years. He loved owning the best things money could buy.

"So how did his dad find out Chip was starting his own business?"

"I'm not sure. It could've been a cop in Big Al's pocket or Emmett. I'm thinking Emmett must have bragged about Chip's operation to someone and that's how it got back to them."

They both startled when they heard the screaming of the police sirens on the roads around the barn. Standing up and peering through the doorway, she watched the police cars with lights flashing make their way down the lane splashing mud up over the vehicles. No wipers swishing the window, so the rain must have subsided.

The two cruisers stopped in front of the door. Lauren waved to them and gave a thumbs up that they were okay. Gary and the other officer emerged from their vehicles. Her heart flipped when she saw Gary walking toward her.

With the recent revelations in her head, Lauren turned to Randy. "It's your decision to come clean with all this information. I won't say a word to them about what you told me." She grabbed his hands.

"I know what I have to do." He gently squeezed her hands. Tears filled his eyes. "I'm sorry. So sorry to put you and Dad through this." He dropped his head. "I'll make it up to you, I promise." His eyes locked on hers. "I'm going to begin by telling the police everything. I want to see DeYoung and Chip and all their cronies behind bars."

Moving back a step, he dropped his arms to his side. His voice choked on the words. "They have to pay for killing Tony."

Chapter Thirty-Two

Gary and his partner met Lauren and Randy at the bottom of the berm. With only thoughts of Lauren's welfare and safety in his mind, and not that he was in uniform and on the job, his long strides carried him to her. He engulfed her in his arms. Yes, she was sopping wet, and his shirt was getting soaked, but he didn't care. He only wanted to know she was alright.

His partner cleared his throat and kicked a rock toward Gary's shoes. With that not-so-gentle reminder that he had work to do, Gary inched back keeping his hands on Lauren's shoulders. Studying her from an arm's length away, relief shot through him when he saw her smile at him. He wished he could pull her close again and capture her mouth with his.

"Are you okay?" He stepped away to scrutinize Randy now.

"Are you both okay?" Gary's gaze shifted from Randy to Lauren.

"We're fine. A whole lot better now you're here." Her weak smile made his stomach clench. If only he could keep her safe in his arms.

"It was Chip," she said. "You've got to find Chip. He's in his truck and he has a shotgun."

The words tumbled out of Lauren so quickly she tripped up on them.

"It came over the radio that Chip's been apprehended with no struggle. They found him in a ditch. He slipped off the road in the rain." Gary arched a brow. "I'm sure he was in a hurry to get out of here. He's in a cruiser on the way to police headquarters, thanks to Randy's 9-1-1 call."

"I don't even remember what I said. I was pretty upset." Randy looked down at his muddy boots.

"So what happened?" Gary tried to appear calm on the outside, but the heat of his concern steamed through his body.

"Randy and I came here to meet Chip." Lauren glanced at Randy.

"It's alright, Lauren." Randy straightened up and faced the police officers. "Chip and I were selling pot." Gary tried not to let his face show his emotion, only to remember he was in uniform and had a job to do. But he couldn't help shake his head as he listened to Randy.

"I wanted out. Chip didn't want me out." Randy blinked and looked at Lauren. She nodded her head.

"He pulled a gun on me. Lauren was supposed to wait in the car." His brow creased into a frown. "But, luckily for me, she didn't. Not so good for her." Shaking his head, he said, "See why I told you to wait in the car, Sis?"

"Please, no sibling squabbles at a time like this. Go on," Gary said.

"Well, when she jumped through the doorway and interrupted us, Chip looked at her and I jumped him. Eventually I got control of the gun, but Chip grabbed Lauren as a shield and tried to escape."

"I was happy to kick him in the nuts to escape from him, but he got away in his truck." She grinned at Gary. "You'll never know how relieved I was to hear you guys stopped him."

"Okay." It took all of Gary's will power not to fold her in is arms.

He tore his gaze from her beautiful face and turned to the officer who accompanied him to the scene. "Let's take a look at the Jeep." The officer nodded and left to get the kits from his cruiser.

Gary caught Lauren's hand in his. He felt a laser-like bolt shoot through his body when he embraced her and felt his strength gentle as she clung to him. He tried to control the quivering in his arms when the realization of the danger she was in hit him. He could have lost her forever.

Stepping away from her, his face sobered. "Do you realize what nearly happened here?"

Her stunning blue eyes rounded. "What do you mean?"

"Chip's a bomb ready to explode. He's a desperate man." Gary stopped, realizing he couldn't reveal anything about the case. "Hopefully we can lock him away for many years along with his father. I don't want Chip around you or released to walk the streets again." The muscle in his jaw tightened. He touched her shoulder. "Do you understand? You can't trust him."

"Oh yes, I know that. He showed how much he cared about me. He was ready to kill me and Randy."

Gary drew her to him and felt her trembling body against his chest. He wished he didn't have to take her back to the police station knowing she would be facing Detective Richards once again.

He edged her face with his hands. "I promise I'll do everything I can to put him behind bars. Believe it."

Chapter Thirty-Three

"Come on let's walk toward the cruisers." In a quieter voice Gary said, "Go slow because we need to talk." He motioned them to begin walking and moved between them, his hand on Randy's arm and his other hand on the small of her back guiding her gently toward the cars. They made their way from the berm and toward the vehicles deliberately picking their steps to avoid the mud puddles and allowing time to talk.

"We're friends and we've been through some great times together. I don't want you to forget that. I want to help you in any way I can." Lauren's heart beat faster. Was it from the exertion of walking through the wet, slippery grass and mud or from the Gary's tender touch?

She could feel the electricity between them vibrate the air. She tried not to stare at his athletic body, wishing she could feel his arms around her. She wanted to plant a big fat kiss on his lips and tell him thank you for promising to get Chip off the street and behind bars.

Lauren looked down to watch her footsteps. She could hear music. Yes, she was humming quietly. When she glanced up, she caught Randy staring at her.

"I'm nervous. Okay?" she shot back at him. He nodded.

"I can tell that, Sis," he said. "You hummed when you were a kid. But this isn't exactly the right time to be humming under your breath." He arched a brow and somehow managed a tiny grin even in the moment when what he had to say to the police would change his life forever.

Her heart almost broke thinking what the consequences of his confession to the crimes could mean for him and for their family. She averted her eyes to the now sunny, blue sky, clamping her lips tight to remind her not to hum.

"What's going to happen now, Gary," Randy asked.

"We'll go back to headquarters to get your statements, but first, as a friend, I want to talk to you about that." He kept a firm grip on Randy's arm as they walked.

"How were you involved in the operation?"

"Well, uh," Randy pulled his shoulders back.

"You don't have to tell me. But I may be able to help you if I know more about your involvement." Gary's eyes narrowed. "I expect you to tell me the truth."

The stillness in the air and the oppressive humidity made Lauren even more uncomfortable realizing the importance of the next life-changing minutes. To hear the truth from Randy made it real. The repercussions of his confession could affect many lives.

Randy stopped. "Okay, the truth is Chip and I were in the process of setting up a drug operation selling the marijuana grown on his property. He had other contacts for cocaine and heroin."

Randy swiped his hand across his forehead to remove the sweat appearing in his hairline. "Lauren had no part in the deal. In fact I didn't want her to come with me today, but, knowing her, I couldn't have stopped her short of hog-tying her to the house."

"That's the truth." Lauren closed the circle by gently squeezing her brother's shoulder and nodded in agreement.

Gary cleared his throat and motioned them to keep walking toward the cruisers. "What was your role in the drug deals?"

"Strictly online sales. Chip wanted me to set up a site on the DarkNet. He never was interested in computers. I love all that technology." He took a breath and continued to talk and walk.

"Wait a minute." Lauren ducked in front of Gary and grabbed Randy's arm to stop him. "What's the DarkNet? That sounds like a kid's sci-fi movie."

"It's like an online black market. People buy drugs, pornography, or even use it as a platform for political protests," Randy said.

Lauren's jaw dropped. "You're making that up. I've never heard of it." She swung her gaze to Gary.

"He's right. Criminals hide their illegal money-making schemes in this relatively unknown part of the Internet."

Lauren twisted to face her brother. "You knew it was illegal. Criminal. And yet, you went along with Chip? What were you thinking?" She thought her head would explode with her pent up anger at her conniving brother.

"He bet me I couldn't do it. So, of course I had to show him I could. At first, it was just a game to me. I never really saw who bought the drugs, never handled them at all. They weren't real to me, like playing a video game. I got a kick out of seeing the sales grow and gloating over the results when I showed the sales to Chip."

They stopped at Gary's cruiser. He turned to look back toward the barn.

Randy's eyes widened. "When I realized this could be a cash cow for us, I began picturing all the things that money could buy and the chance to get out of the funeral business. Chip explained the way we'd split the take. Hell, the way I figured, I'd be rolling in money in six months if I ran the online operation. After that, I guess I wasn't thinking of anything but what Chip promised."

Lauren's anger overwhelmed her. She lunged at Randy and began pummeling his chest with her fists. "Not thinking of the danger, our family, our business." Gary grabbed her flailing arms to stop her and pulled her away from Randy.

"Stop, Lauren." Gary loosened his hold on her after her fury subsided, and she jerked her arms away from his grasp.

"Maybe you should sit in the cruiser and cool off a bit," he said. He opened the back door of the vehicle.

"Oh, no. I want to hear every bit of what he has to say." She glared at Randy and rubbed her arms where Gary had clenched them so tightly.

Placing himself between the siblings, Gary said, "Randy, if you have information about the syndicate's deals across the state lines and the DarkNet connections, the D.A. may cut you a deal."

"Wait a minute. What do you mean?" Lauren's brow furrowed as she turned her attention to Gary.

"Randy could testify against the syndicate's leaders instead of going to jail." Gary shifted his gaze to Randy. "I think the DA would take into consideration your clean record."

Lauren jerked to attention. "Is that possible?"

Randy said, "Well, I know quite a bit about the syndicate behind Chip's contacts." He glanced around the area before he said in a hushed voice, "I'm willing to make a deal if it would mean no jail time."

"I should warn you we can't guarantee the protection, and if they find out you blew the whistle on the syndicate, you'll be a dead man inside of two weeks if you go to jail. You'll have to talk to the DA and the Feds. They may offer you a place in the Witness Protection Program. You'll be given a new identity, re-located..." Gary stopped to take a breath before he continued, "and there will be no more contact with your friends or family."

"Forever?" Randy's voice choked.

"As long as you stay in that program. And in your case, to stay safe, I would say forever."

Randy swallowed hard. "Prison or WPP. Neither one is a good choice."

Lauren covered her middle with her arms. She hated what Randy did, ruining their family, probably ruining their family business. She didn't want Randy to go to prison and she didn't want him to leave forever. Her stomach clenched at the thought of never seeing her brother again.

"Your friend, Tony, was murdered and left in the garage of the funeral home because he was giving us information about the syndicate operations. His dead body was a message to his friends to not even think about ratting on them." Gary said.

Lauren's eyes widened. Hearing the reason Tony was murdered made her stomach flip over. Pressing her arms tighter against her stomach didn't stop the churning inside.

"You'll be a target too once they know you're going to be a witness against them," Gary said to Randy in an even voice. "You'll need protection."

Lauren's hand covered her mouth to smother the cry trying to escape. Staying strong and holding back tears now proved impossible.

Randy dropped his gaze to the wet grass and bowed his head.

"I didn't know. I didn't know Tony gave up information." He shook his head from side to side. "He said he was busted, but the cops let him off 'cause there wasn't enough drugs on him to make it worth the prosecution." His words spilled out of him with a staccato beat. " I was so stupid to believe that!" Randy brushed his hand across his face.

Lauren leaned toward him and rubbed his back to soothe him after hearing such bitter news.

Clenching his hands at his sides, he locked his gaze on Gary. "I want to nail those bastards." His voice throttled by emotion.

"Okay. I'll ask the D.A. to give you a chance to testify against them." Gary put his hand on Randy's shoulder. "I'd recommend you ask for a lawyer to help you negotiate something when you give your statement."

"I don't have a lawyer. Can you suggest someone?"

Gary shook his head. "I can't, but I bet your dad knows who to call."

"What's Dad going to say? My son, who can't do anything right. I need to pull him out of another dumb situation he got himself into." Randy's face reddened. Lauren could hear the bitterness in his voice.

"No, I think he'll be proud to know you're willing to take your punishment, and you're brave enough to stand up to those criminals so they can't hurt any more people." Gary moved in front of Randy. "You're doing the right thing. Trust me."

"Lauren, you'll need to come with me. Say good-bye to Randy. When we get to headquarters, you'll be separated to give your statements and he'll be taken to a safe place. No one will know where he is." The corners of his mouth turned down. "He won't be home again." His grim face signaled the reality of Randy's decision. She turned toward Randy, her hands tented against her lips.

Randy moved to embrace her. He whispered, "It'll be all right. You'll see. It's best for all of us if I do this, Sis."

She squeezed him tightly. "Oh, Randy." Her words wedged in her throat. She didn't want to let go of him, couldn't let go of him. Never see him again? Her tears added more water to his soaked tee shirt. She needed a tissue badly. She pulled away from him and wiped away her tears with her hands to see his face clearly. His eyes filled with moisture, and he scrubbed them away with the heels of his hands.

"We sure make a pair, don't we?" His weak smile didn't light up his red-rimmed eyes. "I'm sorry. So sorry." He flicked his gaze to the sky, and then returned for another hug. "If I don't get to talk to dad, tell him. Please tell him I'm sorry." His words tumbled out between his sobs.

She held onto him more tightly. "I'll tell him." She stepped away, her heart breaking into pieces inside of her. Lauren studied his face taking a mental photo of him to keep in her heart forever. That would be all she'd ever have of him from now on.

Torn between pride for her brother's courage to stand up to the syndicate and with fear for his life, she prayed the police could protect him, realizing that meant she would never know where he was.

Lauren once more locked her arms around his neck. "I love you, Randy. No matter what. Remember that."

Chapter Thirty-Four

After giving her statement at police headquarters, Gary helped Lauren into the police cruiser. Seeing her shaken by the interrogation, he decided not to try small talk with her. He guided the vehicle out of the parking space and made his way onto Main Street. He glanced at Lauren in the passenger seat. Small streaks lined her cheeks from salty tears.

He wished he could wipe her sadness and disappointment away as easily as dabbing away her tears. Only the passing of time could lessen her pain.

Gary couldn't stop thinking about what an idiot Randy was for getting involved in such heinous crime and his anger erupted. He beat the steering wheel with the heel of his hands. "Why the hell did he do it? Why would he consider joining Chip in criminal activities?" He bit his lip to stop. Lauren didn't need to be riled up anymore.

"I wish I knew," she said in a monotone voice. "He always followed Chip's lead, even in grade school" She sighed. "I guess that hasn't changed." She ran her hands through her hair slowly. "I wish I had a better answer."

She covered her face with her hands, her words muffled. "I'm so mad at Randy for doing this to us. Being so stupid. Allowing Chip to manipulate him once again. Breaking our family apart."

Sorry he hadn't controlled his emotions better, he kept his gaze on the road hating to see Lauren in such despair.

Gary breathed deeply to regain his control before he asked, "Do you want me to take you to the funeral home or to your place?"

"The funeral home. I need to explain to Dad what's happened before he hears it from someone else." She turned to face him. "Will you come with me? I don't know how he'll handle all of this. He's lost his wife and now his son within a week."

How could he not stay with her? He wanted to help her through this terrible time. He wanted to give her strength and encouragement. Instead of being the nice guy, standing in the shadows wishing to be with her when they were in high school, it was time for him to step up and step out. He couldn't lose her again.

"Please, Gary, I need you to come with me." Her blue eyes melted away any reserve. Everything in him signaled it was not the best time, but he had to let her know he cared about her. How could he tell her he loved her?

He put his hand out toward her. Heat rushed through him when she grabbed ahold of it. Finally he could tell her, "I'll stay with you forever if you wish."

A smile lit up her entire face. "I'd like that very much."

Their hands rested together on the console between them, and their hearts linked silently.

* * *

"Dad," Lauren yelled as she entered the front door of the funeral home. "Dad, are you here?" She dashed into the foyer. Leaning on the railing of the stairwell, she hollered up the steps. "Dad, are you upstairs?"

No one answered her. She turned a worried frown toward Gary. They hurried toward the family room and looked in. There, slumped on the couch, she saw her father. A bottle of whiskey sat on the end table.

Lauren rushed around the sofa and crouched in front of him. Grabbing his hands, she asked, "Are you all right." The pungent smell of alcohol attacked her senses.

He blinked up at her. "I couldn't be better. My wife's gone and my son..." His words slurred together.

"Mr. Staab, I think we all need a cup of coffee. Right, Lauren?" Gary headed toward the coffee maker as Lauren settled herself on the couch next to her dad.

"I need more than a cup of coffee, a lot stronger than coffee."

"Well, it looks to me like you've had plenty of strong stuff, Dad."

He sat up straight. "Are you sayin' I'm drunk?"

"Yeah. Have you been drinking since we left? It smells like a bar in here. I hope nobody's stopped by to see you like this."

He thought a minute before shaking his head. "Nope. Nobody's been here, at least I don't think so." He took another swig from his glass and spoke over the rim, "No one will ever want to come here again."

Lauren took the glass and set it on the table. "You've had enough. Gary's making coffee and then we can talk. Okay?"

"Hell, I might as well go pee if I have to wait for the coffee." He rocked up off the couch and swayed. Lauren jumped up to steady him.

"I'm fine." She let go of his arm and he stumbled toward the bathroom. He took a few steps forward and a few back. Gary strode across the room to help him, but her dad waved off his help. "I've been takin' care of business all my life. I don't need your help!"

Gary backed off and let him pass.

"He's a stubborn guy." Lauren smiled at Gary. "He'll be all right."

She approached Gary. "He has to deal with all this mess in his own way."

Gary reached around her and pulled her close to him. She didn't care if she finished her thought about her dad or not. Finally, she could wriggle into his arms, take in the masculine scent of him, and gain the strength to survive this scandal. She looked up into his face and studied his brown eyes full of gentleness. He tipped her chin toward him and kissed her deeply. A high powered-current blazed through her body as she reveled in the kiss.

Gary pulled away for a minute, and she caught her breath. He cupped her face in his hands. "I know this is a crazy time for you. I want to help get you through all of it." His face was so close to hers. She couldn't resist touching his cheek and tracing his bristly chin with her finger.

She caught his sultry gaze and pressed her lips to his. His tongue tickled her lips and a delicious tingling feathered its way up her arms.

He moved back a step, catching her face in his fingertips. "I love you," he said in a husky voice.

Placing her fingers around his wrists, she whispered, "I love you too."

He caressed her neck, ran his hands over her shoulders and across her back. Again they embraced and exhilaration filled the center of her heart.

They didn't release each other even after her father cleared his throat loud enough for the whole world to hear.

"Um, I'm sorry. I didn't mean to break this up. I can leave." He leaned against the coffee bar countertop for support.

Slowly they stepped away from each other and turned toward her dad. "No need to leave. We have our whole lives ahead of us, together."

Her father's face brightened and his eyes widened. "Well, that's a good thing to come out of this day." He was a bit rocky as he made his way back to the sofa and eased onto the cushions. "Now where's that coffee? I want to know about my son."

Chapter Thirty-Five

Lauren brought the steaming coffee mug to her dad and sat next to him on the couch. She watched as he gingerly sipped the hot brew.

His faded eyes sought Lauren's. "I got a call from Randy, from jail. What the hell?"

His voice was loud. He looked at her with the eyes she remembered when she had come in late on a date. The truth was the only thing he wanted to hear.

"Mr. Staab."

Her dad interrupted. "I think since you're mooning over my daughter, you can call me Jensen, unless, of course, you're here on official police business. But from what I saw, it was not police business."

Gary smiled. "Fine." Amusement sparkled in his eyes.

"Yuck," Jensen said as he placed the coffee on the end table next to the couch. "Give me some more whiskey." He eyed Lauren with his most persuasive face.

"You're okay, Dad. You're already looking more sober. Take a few more sips of coffee."

Jensen shook his head and directed his gaze to Gary. "Now tell me what's going to happen to Randy. I hoped that he would come home with you." His eyes glistened with tears. "I only talked with him a few minutes, but I know..." His shaky voice trailed off into mumbled words. His gaze went to Lauren as he clamped his mouth shut.

"He'll be held in protective custody until trial because he's ready to talk with police about the syndicate and testify against them so they can round up the big players," Gary said.

"Did Randy call you to get a name for a defense lawyer," Lauren asked.

Her dad nodded. "I called Jack Hargrove, my lawyer, who will get in touch with a criminal lawyer. They'll make the arrangements and hammer out some kind of an agreement." His eyes flashed. "I want Randy out of here. He'll be dead the minute he hits the streets otherwise."

"The D.A, will offer him the Witness Protection Program. They'll keep him safe," Gary said in a reassuring voice hoping that the D.A. would actually agree to allow Randy's testimony.

Lauren sat next to her father on the couch and touched his hand. "But, Dad, he won't be able to contact us as long as he's in the WPP."

Jensen bent over, elbows on his knees, and kneading his temples. "If I had listened to Barbara all those years ago, my son would never be in this position." His voice cracked with emotion.

"What do you mean?" Lauren twisted her body toward her dad.

He sat up to face her. "Your mother told me Al DeYoung was a gangster. He was in the syndicate, a wise guy, she called him. Al murdered Henry by running him off the road just as sure as the sun'll shine tomorrow."

Lauren's eyes widened in surprise.

Gary looked confused. "Who's Henry? I haven't heard anything like that."

Jensen sucked in a deep breath. "Henry was Al's trusted accountant. He found out all about the drug operation when he kept the books for the farm."

"So Henry was part of the drug rings so many years ago," Gary asked. "Was he planning on going to the police with information?"

Her dad raised an eyebrow. "Yes, in fact he was an FBI agent collecting evidence against the mob. It took years for him to gain Al and his cohorts' confidence.

Lauren stood up and leaned toward her dad. "You knew all this, but you never told the police?" Her voice pitched higher.

Jensen sat back in the couch. "Yes, but I couldn't tell the police because the mob would find out who snitched on them and would come after your mother."

"But if he was working for DeYoung, he must've been reporting everything to the police. Why didn't they nail DeYoung for Henry's murder," Gary asked.

"There was no way DeYoung would get his hands dirty. He hired a killer, and he was probably out of town minutes after running

Henry off the road. No link to Big Al." Jensen dropped his hands into his lap. "That and a cover-up by the police department I'm sure," Jensen muttered.

"Do you have any evidence to put behind that statement?" Gary folded his arms across his chest.

"No, but there wasn't any investigation. They closed it out as an accident due to the wet roads. I always suspected a cover up." Jensen lowered his gaze to the floor.

Gary shook his head. "Wait a minute. I'm lost here. Why would Henry confide in your wife?"

Jensen sliced his gaze to Lauren and back to Gary. "My wife and Henry had a special close relationship. He revealed what was happening at the farm and eventually admitted he was working undercover there."

"Why would he do that? He's a professional. That undercover identity is never exposed." Gary's face creased with incredulity. "I don't understand it."

"Because my mother was in love with Henry." Lauren's voice colored with disdain. She shifted her gaze away from Gary and locked on her father. "Wasn't she, Dad?" She waited a minute for a reply, but Jensen seemed speechless. She practically spat out her next statement. "And lovers reveal all their secrets to each other."

Her dad's eyes opened wide. "Lauren, I didn't realize you knew…" He slumped into the couch.

Lauren's lips formed a thin, tight line. She had rehearsed different ways to ask her Dad about her mother and Henry's affair, trying to achieve a reasonable way to approach him without an angry confrontation. But those rehearsals were useless. She had failed when erupting with the accusation hoping against hope he would deny it. Eager to dispel the fact that her ideal childhood had been a sham, she wanted the affair to be a fairy tale, just as unbelievable as conjuring up a shadow man.

Her hand went to the heart necklace around her neck. The chain felt hot and heavy on her bare skin. The necklace was real. She grabbed the heart and held it. Her eyes searched the room for a sign of her mother.

"I heard her talk about Henry while she was in the nursing home once in a while. I didn't know if he was real or imaginary." Clasping the heart pendant, she hoped she was a good enough actress to pull off this lie.

Yes she'd heard her mother talking about Henry. But she had also talked *to* Henry. Even if she didn't want to believe she had seen Henry with her mother, she knew for sure he was real and their love was real. The symbol of their love was in her hand.

Squeezing her eyes tight, the niggling question almost flowed out to her father. *Am I the result of their love affair?* She could not

240

confront him now with that question. Not when he had to deal with losing his wife and his son, Randy, forever.

"I'm afraid that's true." Her dad glanced down to the floor, and then looked up at Lauren. "We had some tough times." He sighed. "I admit I paid more attention to the business than I did to her. I lost her."

"But she came back to you, Dad." Lauren sat down beside her father, her arm on the back of the couch, and turned so she could meet his eyes.

"She told me Henry was leaving because he got word that DeYoung was tipped off about him being undercover. He wanted her to go with him. That night he was murdered."

Lauren gulped back a cry to stop the story, but she needed to know the truth. She scooted closer to her dad and linked her arm through his.

"That was the night she admitted to me he had asked her to go away with him. She always believed if he had left sooner, instead of staying and trying to convince her to leave with him, he wouldn't have been murdered."

Jensen took a deep breath as he reached for Lauren's hand. "She refused to go with him because she couldn't abandon you and your brother and me." He brushed tears from his eyes.

"We had some tough times, but we had a history together. She wasn't willing to throw it all away. We worked it out." He reached for her hand and held it. "I loved that woman. She was

241

my treasure." His eyes glistened with tears. "The Alzheimer's took her from me way before her death. I miss her every day."

"I know, Dad. So do I." She wrapped her arms around him and held on. She didn't need to know if she were his biological daughter. He truly was her father, the guy who loved and protected her all through her childhood and now into her adult years. He would always be her father. That was all she needed.

Lauren let go of her dad to scrub away the pool of tears collected in her eyes. Gary moved toward her with some tissue.

She took the offered tissue and dabbed at her eyes and nose. Taking in a ragged breath, she patted the sofa cushion next to her.

Gary slipped in next to her on the couch and put his arm around her shoulders. She felt her heart warm with the love radiating from these two men she loved with all her heart.

Epilogue

Lauren gazed around the front room of the funeral home. The morning sunlight filtered through the sheer panels of the east windows adding cheer to the space, even if the day would be one filled with tears.

Floral tributes arranged along the opposite wall softened the front room which was converted into the funeral chapel for her mother's celebration of life. Folding chairs placed in straight rows sat ready for the invited guests to arrive and recorded music was loaded into the player. Lauren remembered her mother's attention to all the details before a funeral service. She smiled thinking of her and her insistence on even having a glass of water ready for the clergy leading the service.

Once again, her mother's best friend, Norma, had been the one she had relied on to help prepare for the gathering. Truly a friend to the family, Norma had been with them through all the trying times since her mother had been diagnosed with Alzheimer's. She had been the support and comfort for Lauren and her father through the nightmare of the murder investigation, Randy's arrest, and the scandal it created.

As she gazed across the room filled with the antiques her mother had searched out for the Victorian décor, she caught a glimpse of a movement near her. *Henry.* She had been too pre-occupied to notice the room cool and the tickle in her nose.

"Henry, I know you're here." She brought the tissue to her nose and caught the three quick sneezes in it.

"Yes, I'm here with you, dear Lauren."

She turned and saw the apparition of the handsome young man in the suit and tie standing near the table with her mother's photo and flowers placed on it.

Lauren's face lighted up in delight. "I was hoping you would be here. Mom isn't with you?"

"No, she thought it would be rather awkward to come to her own funeral." He winked. "And she didn't know how uncomfortable you would be with the situation."

"Oh, yes, it would be a bit awkward as you say." She nodded. "Tell her thanks. But I do hope she'll visit another time."

Lauren laughed out loud. "I would hate to see my mom making faces at me during the eulogies."

Henry's rumbling chuckle broke through the still room. "You're so right about that! She's a very special lady."

"Yes, she is. I hope people will remember her for being a great mom, all the worthwhile projects she did for our church and community

244

and not for her last years stricken with Alzheimer's disease."

Henry hovered closer to her. "She wasn't the woman we all knew after she got sick. People realize that disease robs us of the real person."

"I know, but it's so hard." The rock in her throat wouldn't allow her to talk. Blinking away her tears, she stopped trying to say anything out loud. She could only communicate with her thoughts picked up by Henry.

Lauren felt her anxiety melt away as she looked into her birth father's eyes. She felt she was looking into her own eyes.

"I'm glad you realized Gary truly is your Lover Boy. He's a keeper," Henry said.

A surge of warmth radiated through her body just thinking about him. "And you knew that all along, didn't you?"

"Well...I have some inside information from another world that helps me know these things." The corners of his mouth tugged up into a handsome smile.

"Your friends are coming now, Lauren."

She heard the front door open. "Okay. I'd better go and greet them." She blew a kiss to Henry, and he blew one back to her.

Turning toward the entry way, she squared her shoulders and strode to the door.

Her best friends, Stephanie and Piper, entered through the heavy door and immediately grabbed her to share loving hugs. Each of them had been her rock as she faced all the turmoil in her life since first grade. They had shepherded her through the rough days following Randy's arrest and were there for her on this emotional day too.

Lauren blinked back the tears and took a deep breath as she greeted more friends and family and showed them into the front room of the funeral home.

She was glad she and her father had waited to have the funeral until Randy had given his testimony to the judge. They needed time to adjust to her mother's death and Randy's absence. She used the time to focus on her mother's life and to work through the reasons for hiding the truth about Henry from her for so long.

Lauren was grateful to have the support of those friends and family who attended this afternoon's service. Checking once more if everyone was finding seats, she realized not one of Randy's friends showed up.

As she turned toward the table graced with her mother's photo, she noticed the photo was now placed between the floral arrangement from her family and a similar arrangement of white carnations.

Her brow furrowed with wonder over why Norma would place those flowers on that table honoring her mother. Only family pieces should be there. Her eyes widened with the realization that white carnations were her mother's favorite flowers. Who else would know that?

She strode to the table and pulled the card from the holder. "Love." There was no signature, only a drawing of a tic-tac-toe board, the game she and Randy played, fought over when one lost, gloated about when one claimed victory. Tears stung her eyes.

She wanted to hug that card. The flowers had to be from Randy. But how did they get here? He was hidden at a secret location for his protection with strict orders not to contact anyone.

Lauren turned to peruse the room of guests. Gary. Would he have connections to get in contact with Randy?

She caught Norma's glance at her from where she sat in one of the chairs. Norma flipped her gaze away quickly but returned to focus on Lauren. She flashed that mischievous smile with a puckish sparkle in her eyes. How could Norma manage it?

She didn't care who arranged the flowers to be at the service. Her heart was filled with joy and relief knowing Randy was safe, and he was all right.

She turned back to the flowers and inhaled the fresh, spicy fragrance of the carnations. Three tiny sneezes escaped her. Why would she sneeze when she had breathed in the real thing, definitely not Henry's signal he was present. Or was he?

The shadow skimming across her view confirmed Henry truly was still here with her. A blanket of comfort fell across her shoulders.

A tap on her shoulder and Lauren jumped. "Sorry, I didn't mean to scare you." Her dad was next to her.

"Oh, you surprised me, that's all." She motioned to the carnations on the table. "Did you see these flowers are from Randy?"

"Yes. I don't know how he did it, but I'm glad he did. I miss him here today." Tears formed in his eyes. "That kid had a hard time growing up into a man. But I believe he's on the right track now. He owned up to his part in the crimes and helped to put those guys behind bars." Her dad grabbed a clean handkerchief from his back pocket and wiped his eyes. "I love him." His voice choked.

"Me too." She slipped her arm through her dad's.

"Are we ready to begin the service?"

Her father nodded and escorted her to the front row of chairs to join the seated guests. Gary stood as she approached her chair and reached for her hand. His touch strengthened her as she sat down between her dad and Gary.

Lauren was ready to accept the reality of her life now. She was prepared to say good-bye to the life with her mother on this earth and look forward to a future with Gary.

* * *

The quiet of the evening with only the chirping sounds of crickets was a time of peace for Lauren. She and Gary stood in silence on the patio outside of her duplex, their arms around each other's waists. The light summer breeze scented with the fragrance of freshly mown grass ruffled her hair.

Gary pulled her closer. "What are you thinking," he asked in a soft voice.

Lauren sighed and turned to face him. "I'mwondering if Randy is looking at this gorgeous sky filled with the constellations. He knew them all."

Gary touched her temple, her cheek, and chin, tilting her face up to him. "I imagine he's doing just fine. Probably thinking about you too." He brushed his lips across hers. Lauren's heart thrummed with desire. She slipped her hands to the sides of his face and pulled him to her basking in the luxury of a deeper kiss.

"Hey, wait a minute." She stepped away from Gary and couldn't stop smiling at the surprised look on his face.

"What?" His arms opened wide.

"I believe you need to explain how Randy was able to get those flowers sent to the funeral today. No more hugging, kissing, touching till I get an answer." She shook her finger at him with every word.

"Now you know I can't tell you." He folded his arms across his chest. A boyish grin lighted up his face.

"Aha, so it *was* you! And what did Norma have to do with it?"

"Norma is innocent. Nothing." His sober face, but impish eyes, gave him away.

"You know Norma will tell me all about it, don't you?" She moved closer to him. "So you might as well 'fess up to it." She ran her hands across his shoulders and down his arms.

"Hold on there. I thought you said no touching till you find out."

She winked. "I lied." Reaching for him, she snuggled into his hard chest, and he enfolded her in his arms.

"We'll have a lifetime together for you to figure it out," he said in a husky voice as he hugged her tighter.

A lifetime together. Lauren glanced at the starry heavens above. A lifetime and more.

The End

IF YOU ENJOYED THIS BOOK, PLEASE LEAVE A REVIEW.

J.Q. Rose from Books We Love

Terror on Sunshine Boulevard
Dangerous Sanctuary

J Q Rose is an avid reader, photographer, and blogger with blogs about the writing process and growing a vegetable garden. Janet and her husband are snowbirds who spend winters in Florida allowing them to garden twelve months out of the year. Summer finds her up north camping and hunting toads, frogs, and salamanders with her grandchildren.

Connect online with J.Q. Rose at:

J.Q. Rose blog

http://www.jqrose.com/

Facebook

http://facebook.com/jqroseauthor

bwlpublishing.ca